THE DOLL'S ALPHABET

Camilla Grudova lives in Toronto. She holds a degree in Art History and German from McGill University, Montreal. Her fiction has appeared in *The White Review* and *Granta*.

Fitzcarraldo Editions

THE DOLL'S ALPHABET

CAMILLA GRUDOVA

CONTENTS

UNSTITCHING

One afternoon, after finishing a cup of coffee in her living room, Greta discovered how to unstitch herself. Her clothes, skin and hair fell from her like the peeled rind of a fruit, and her true body stepped out. Greta was very clean so she swept her old self away and deposited it in the rubbish bin before even taking notice of her new physiognomy, the difficulty of working her new limbs offering no obstruction to her determination to keep a clean home.

She did not so much resemble a sewing machine as she was the ideal form on which a sewing machine was based. The closest thing she resembled in nature was an ant.

She admired herself in the mirror for a short time then went to see her neighbour Maria, across the hall in her building. When Maria saw Greta, she was not afraid for she suddenly recognized herself. She knew that she looked the same inside, and could also unstitch herself, which she did, unashamed, in front of Greta.

They admired each other, and ate almond cake as they did every afternoon, but now using their newly discovered real mouths, which were framed by steely, sharp black mandibles which felt like a pleasant cross between teeth and a moustache.

When Greta's husband came home he was horrified. He had never touched her sewing machine before – it frightened him – and he would certainly not touch Greta's newly discovered body.

She moved across the hall to live with Maria, who was a widow and no longer had a husband to frighten. She brought her sewing machine with her.

Their sewing machines were not used but kept around

the house, decoratively, the way they used to keep saint figurines and dolls, and the way grander people kept marble portrait busts of themselves.

They were a sensation the first time they left the building to do their shopping. After seeing other women unstitched, it was impossible not to do it, and soon all the women in their neighbourhood had shed their skins.

It brought great relief to unstitch, like undoing one's brassiere before bedtime or relieving one's bladder after a long trip.

Men were divided between those who 'always knew there was something deceitful about women' and were therefore satisfied when they were proved right, and those who lamented 'the loss of the female form'. There was also a small minority of men who tried to unstitch themselves with the aid of razorblades and knives, only to end up wounded and disappointed. They had no 'true, secret' selves inside, only what was taught and known.

On the unstitched bodies of women, there were various small hoops, almost like pierced ears, through which a red thread continually flowed, speeding or slowing, depending on the individual's mood. It was a thick, tough thread covered in a wax-like substance.

On each woman, the hoops were in slightly different places and of various sizes but, otherwise, all the women looked alike.

After the unstitching, sewing machines were no longer used; the act of using one, of stitching things together, was seen as a form of repression, an outdated distraction women used to deny themselves unstitching, and so sewing machines took on a solely formal, aesthetic role, beautiful in their quiet stillness.

Exhibitions of sewing and sewing machines 'throughout the ages' were put on and greatly enjoyed, reminding women of their evolution towards unstitching consciousness.

THE MOUSE QUEEN

Our apartment always looked like Christmas because the shelves were laden with red and green Loeb books in Greek and Latin. Peter's uncle gave him one every year for his birthday, and we had bought more from second hand shops. Whenever we had guests over, Peter had to point out that he had covered the English translation side of the Latin books with sheets of coloured paper. He and I met in Latin class at university. I was drawn to Latin because it didn't belong to anybody, there were no native speakers to laugh at me. There were private school kids in my classes who had studied Latin before, but I quickly overtook them. Peter, who was one of them, slicked his hair back like a young Samuel Beckett and had the wet, squinting look of an otter.

He looked down on Philosophy and Classics students who planned to go into law. Under his influence, so did I. Peter wore the same type of clothes every day: heavy striped shirts from an army surplus store, sweaters that hadn't been dried properly after washing, khakis, Doc Martens and a very old-fashioned cologne whose scent vaguely resembled chutney. He had bought the cologne at a yard sale, only about a teaspoon had been used by the previous owner. It wasn't until we had dated for some time that I learned his parents were lawyers, that he had grown up with much more money than I had.

Peter and I were married in a church with a replica of Michelangelo's *Pietà*. We only invited one friend, an English major who loved Evelyn Waugh, as we thought he was the only person we knew who would understand we wanted to be married in such a manner. Of course our parents wouldn't want us to be married so young – before we had jobs – so we didn't tell them at all. We didn't move in together until our last semester of university, into an apartment above an abandoned grocery store. The landlord had stopped running it years before and left it as it was, with a faded 'Happy Canada Day' poster and popsicle advertisements on the dusty glass windows. It was cheap for a one-bedroom, because not many people wanted to live above an abandoned but unemptied grocery store – the threat of vermin seemed too much, and the landlord just couldn't bring himself to clean it and do something with the space. It seemed he thought he might open it again some time in the future, to sell the mouldy chocolate bars and hardened gum that remained there.

There was a hatch in our floor that led to a back room in the shop downstairs, and into the shop itself. Down there, Peter found some old cigarettes which seemed safe in comparison to all the old food, and newspapers that dated from when we were five years old. In our living room we had a parlour organ that had belonged to his grandfather. Peter loved the organ – it was a much, much older instrument than the piano. Organs were invented in the Hellenistic period. They were powered using water. In Ancient Rome, Nero played such an organ.

On the organ's mantel, Peter put a plaster model of a temple which fits in the palm of one's hand, a statue of Minerva bought at an Italian shop, a collection of postcards of nude athletes Peter got from the British Museum, and a large framed copy of Botticelli's portrait of St Augustine. Sometimes I was woken up in the middle of the night by the sound of Peter playing the organ, wearing nothing but his bathrobe, his hair in his face.

We turned a little chair too rickety to sit on into an altar. We made a collage of saints and Roman gods, a mixture of pictures and statues, and oddly shaped candles we had picked up here and there – beehives, trees, cones, owls, angels. Sometimes Peter left offerings, grapes, little cups full of wine and, to my dismay, raw chicken breasts and other bits of meat he bought at a butcher's. A friend told us it was dangerous to worship such a large, mixed crowd.

After graduating, we planned to live cheaply and save up to move to Rome. We both thought there was no point in applying to graduate school unless we first spent a period of time in Rome researching something original to write about.

In the meantime, I found work in a doll's house shop. We sold tiny things to put in them, from lamps to Robert Louis Stevenson books with real, microscopic words in them. Peter got a job in a graveyard, installing tombstones, digging graves, helping with Catholic burial processes, and cleaning up messes. He would find diaphragms, empty bottles of spirits, squirrel skins left over from hawks' meals, and dozens of umbrellas. He brought the umbrellas home, until our apartment started to look like a cave of sleeping bats. I had an umbrella yard sale one Saturday when he was at work:

ALL UMBRELLAS TWO DOLLARS AS IS

It was an overcast day so I did well for myself.

Peter was sombre-looking and strong so everyone thought him ideal, and his Latin came in useful. He was outdoors most of the time. He developed a permanent sniffle, and smelled like rotting flowers and cold stones. There was a mausoleum that was a perfect, but smaller replica of a Greek temple – Peter spent his lunch breaks smoking, reading, and eating sandwiches on the steps.

It was built by the founder of a grand department store that sold furs, uncomfortably scratchy blankets, shoes and other things. Peter threw his cigarette butts through a gated window leading into the mausoleum, as he didn't think such a man deserved a classical temple. He was half driven mad by the cemetery – 'a dreadful facsimile of Rome', he called it – but couldn't afford to leave. It paid very well because not many people were morbid and solemn enough to stand working in a cemetery. The owner said Peter was very dignified and he could see him going far in the cemetery business.

We both put up advertisements – 'LATIN TUTORS AVAILABLE' – in bookstores and libraries, but received no replies.

Living together we became careless compared to how we normally acted with each other, and a few months after graduating I discovered I was pregnant. When I started to show, I was fired; the owner of the doll's house shop thought I would bump into all the precious little things with my new bulk and break them. I felt like a doll's house myself, with a little person inside me, and imagined swallowing tiny chairs and pans in order for it to be more comfortable.

When we learned we were having twins, Peter said the ultrasound photo looked like an ancient, damaged frieze. As I grew larger, I wore pashmina shawls around the house, tied around my body like tunics.

Neither of us had twins in our families. It was the Latin that did it, Peter said, did I have any dreams of swans or bearded gods visiting me? He acted like I had betrayed him in a mythological manner. I had dreams that Trajan's column and the Pantheon grew legs and chased me which I didn't tell him about, as I thought they would upset him further.

One night Peter didn't come home from the grave-yard. He arrived at dawn, covered in mud, his coat off and bundled under his arm. He opened the coat, inside was the corpse of a very small woman, a dwarf I suppose. She wore a black Welsh hat like Mother Goose, it was glued to her head. She had black buckled shoes and a black dress with white frills along the hem, wrists and neck, and yellow stockings. Her face was heavily painted, to look very sweet, but her eyelids had opened, though she was dead.

We buried a small, black coffin today, said Peter, I thought it was so terrible, the eternal pregnancy of death. If we are to have two, what difference will three make, he said, and laughed horribly, like a donkey. He had never laughed like that before. I dug the coffin up again, took her out and put the coffin back empty, he said, no one will know.

Peter stumbled off to bed, leaving me with the little corpse. Her eyeballs looked horrible. I thought I would turn to stone if I looked at them too long. I threw Peter's coat in the bathtub, wrapped her in a sheet, put her in a garbage bag. Then I picked her up. She was extraordinarily heavy. I decided I would stuff her in the organ, it was the only good hiding place but I had the horrible thought that it would become haunted with her, and the keys would play her voice.

I brought her down to the grocery store, and put her behind the counter. She was heavy. I hoped if she stayed there long enough she would shrink like an apple, and Peter could bring her back to the graveyard well hidden in a purse and rebury her like a bulb.

I kept thinking about her eyes, and later returned downstairs to put pennies over them. The pennies didn't cover the whole of them, they were very large eyes, but I didn't want to waste one- or two-dollar coins.

Peter slept for twenty hours. When he woke up, he didn't remember what he had done, so I didn't tell him. As he recovered his accusations against my pregnancy redoubled: I had consorted with ancient pagan gods. He sat in the bathtub with no water in it, reading St Augustine and burning incense. He left for Mass on Sundays without me. We had our own odd version of Catholicism where we went to a different Catholic church every Sunday, while on sporadic Sundays we went to a large park that was mostly forest and took off our clothes and drew crosses on ourselves with mud as Peter muttered incantations. I never knew which church he was going to. I stayed home and read my favourite passages from *The Metamorphoses*.

He boiled our marriage certificate in the tea kettle, saying he wouldn't work in a cemetery for the rest of his life just to feed the children of Mars and, finally, he left, while I was at the grocery store buying him lettuce and coffee.

When I came home, his bulky green leather suitcase, which reminded me of a toad, was gone, as were a selection of the Loeb books, the jar of Ovaltine, and my favourite purple wool cardigan which was too small for me to wear with my pregnant belly. He had left all his underwear, most likely out of forgetfulness, and they stared at me like the haughty, secretive heads of white Persian cats when I opened the clothes drawer.

I found his parents' address on an old report card. I had never met them. The house was in the suburbs, I had to take a train there. There weren't any sidewalks, only lawns and roads. I passed a frightening house with a sagging porch. Between the door and the window there was a rotting moose's head on a plaque. The moose winked at me. The movement caused the moose's glass eyeball to fall out and roll across the porch and onto the lawn.

It was a very large fake Tudor house, the white parts were grimy, and there was a bathtub on the lawn, used as a planter for carnations. There were two very old black Cadillacs parked in the drive, probably from the 1980s. I had grown up in an apartment with only a mother who didn't know how to drive. It was Peter's mother who answered the door, I knew it was her because she also resembled an otter, her grey hair slicked back from her face. She wore a very old-fashioned looking purple suit, and grimaced at my stomach.

I asked her if Peter was there, and she said no, he had gone to the States for law school, she was glad he was finally getting himself together.

I left, feeling sick, imagining the babies swimming in my stomach like otters, with the faces of Peter and his mother. I ran back to the train station, not caring if the motion killed the foetuses. Back downtown, I wondered what it would be like to be run over by a tram – perhaps like being pushed through a sewing machine.

I didn't have enough money to pay the rent the next month. I hoped the landlord would forget me the way he forgot his grocery store, but he came a few days before the month was up and asked for cheques for the next three months in advance as he was going to Wales to visit his cousin.

I had to leave all the furniture and the organ, we couldn't afford to rent movers. I scooped all the stuff off the organ's mantel and dumped it in my purse. My mother scolded me when I tried to pack Peter's clothes and other things. He hadn't taken his razor, his galoshes or his long maroon scarf. My mother and I took what

21

we could box by box, on the tram, and once in a cab, my arms weighed down with plastic bags filled with Loeb books. I was glad to leave the old dead woman, whom I hadn't had a chance to check on.

My mother lived in a dark, ground-floor apartment, she had moved after I started university, to a smaller place. It only had one bedroom, so I had to stay on the couch. All the furniture was blue and green brocade, and there were trinkets I remembered from childhood: a wooden horse missing its two back legs, a paper clown in a music box which started to dance when you opened a little drawer on the bottom, a model ship covered in dust, a collection of toy donkeys I was never allowed to play with because they had belonged to my grandfather, and all sorts of things bought at yard sales, discount shops and in Chinatown – baskets, pincushions, back-scratchers, plastic flowers, peacock feathers. It was a horrible thing that you could buy peacock feathers for less than a dollar.

There was no room for all my Loeb books, I had to put them underneath the couch where they became all dusty.

When I was little, my mother had given me a department store catalogue to read. It was full of toys I couldn't have, but I could cut out the pictures, she told me, she had already looked through the catalogue. I was amazed by a set of twin dolls: how did they manage to make them exactly the same? My mother laughed at me and said there were hundreds of them made in a factory, and everything else I owned had identical siblings, that's how the world was now.

I was couch-ridden for a month after having the twins. I felt like Prometheus, the babies were eagles with soft beaks, my breasts being continually emptied and filled.

I didn't name them Romulus and Remus as Peter and I had planned – Peter thought we simply couldn't name them anything else – but Aeneas and Arthur.

My mother looked after the twins when I was well enough to look for work. She left them in strange places, under tables and in cupboards, but they weren't old enough to attend day care. I couldn't go back to the doll's house shop, the owner was more interested in a fake pristine, miniature domestic life – unused pots and pans, cradles without babies in them. She didn't even like to have children in her shop, her ideal customers were older men and women like herself, who wore brooches and would spend hundreds of dollars on a tiny imitation Baroque chair. I was too embarrassed to go looking around the university for work, or to put up any signs offering Latin tutoring – I felt like I had given birth to the twins from my head and my head hadn't recovered.

The air in my mother's neighbourhood was always sickly sweet because of a chocolate factory, and it was there I got a job. All the chocolates were sold in purple and gold packaging. Fruits, nuts, and other things were delivered and encased in chocolate, the opened boxes looked like displays of shells, eggs and rocks in a natural history museum. From my first day working there, I had nightmares of eating chocolates filled with bird bones, rocks, gold nuggets, Roman coins, teeth.

There was one other person with a university degree at the factory, a girl named Susan who studied English but couldn't find a job in that field and had a child. She had named her daughter Charlotte Fitzgerald after Charlotte Brontë and F. Scott Fitzgerald. She was a horrible, large child who carried a headless plastic doll everywhere with her, and spat into its body like an old man who chewed on tobacco. Her spit was always brown because Susan gave her sweets from the factory. Charlotte Fitzgerald was six, and didn't know how to read. She threw tantrums if Susan didn't give her sweets. I liked Susan but didn't want my babies to spend too much time with Charlotte in case she influenced them. I never took home any free chocolates. I knew my mother would like them, but I also knew she would give some to Aeneas and Arthur when I wasn't there, and sugar was like a nasty potion that would turn them into monsters. Susan often told me you could only have a limited influence on how your kids turned out, she felt Charlotte was already ruined and wished she hadn't been born. I tried to pick out the nicest toys at second-hand shops, I stayed away from garish plastic things, I took lots of books out of the library for them but they were too young to read them and ripped them apart. They learned all sorts of things I couldn't control at day care, words like 'gosh'. Once, as I read them *Aesop's Fables* translated into Latin, one of them yelled 'Batman' at me.

As they didn't have a father, I bought a male doll wearing a suit and bowtie with a string coming out of his back which, when pulled, emitted a laugh, but the laugh didn't take long to stop working, and his grin bothered me so I threw him out, longing for sombre and cruel Peter.

I saved up enough money to find a place of my own when the twins were almost two years old. It looked like a house from the outside, but was really just one small room with a bathroom built in an old closet, a concrete yard and a little fence that didn't reach my knees. There was no bathtub, only a shower, and I had to buy a plastic bin to wash the babies in. There was a tile depicting St Francis on the front of the house, beside the door.

I thought of Peter all the time. I took the twins for

walks in the cemetery where he used to work, though the stroller was hard to push over grass. Whenever I saw cigarette butts, I imagined they were his. I collected umbrellas, and sold them from my front door on my days off. I also walked by our old apartment. The grocery store was still the same, and I imagine our rooms upstairs were too – the parlour organ, the bed now stripped of blankets, the shelves with no books on them – and of course the shrivelled old lady downstairs behind the counter.

I tried to remind myself of all the times Peter acted horribly: just after we moved in together, we decided to have a costume party. I wanted to dress up as Argus from *The Metamorphoses*. I bought a white dress and painted eyes all over it, as well as a pair of white gauze wings which I also turned into eyes. When I tried my costume on a few days before the party, Peter said I looked terrifying, and everyone would think I was maddeningly jealous and controlling of him and he wouldn't be able to enjoy himself. I threw the costume out, and decided to be a mouse from *The Nutcracker* instead of anything from Greek and Roman mythology. Peter didn't know anything about ballets or Tchaikovsky and neither did I, really. I had seen a production of *The Nutcracker* as a child and I remembered it as all blurry with a cardboard sleigh and fake snow. I bought a grey leotard, crinoline, and made a mouse tail, ears out of paper.

Peter decided to be a lamppost. It was quite awful, he painted his face yellow, with a red and blue line across the centre of his face, and made a kind of black paper lantern to wear over his head – it looked more like a bird cage. And he wore a black shirt with frills which he thought resembled the arabesques on some old European streetlights. I was baffled as to why he chose to be a lamp and was so enthusiastic about it, though I knew he thought dressing up as historical figures vulgar: he was furious when someone showed up as St Francis, wearing a dirty brown tunic with fake birds sewn onto it.

A girl dressed up as the full moon kept trying to kiss Peter. She smelled like talcum powder and unwashed stockings, which is how I imagined the moon to smell. For the party, Peter had bought tins of snails, they smelled nasty, and floated in grey water. Why did he have to waste money on them when there were snails in the shed behind our building? The Romans enjoyed snails, he said to me in an irritable voice. He arranged them decoratively on bits of lettuce, that's all there was to eat, besides the punch we made and some saltine crackers.

Lots of people came, and there were, I realized, many rich girls from our university who had grown up doing ballet. I was so afraid of them asking me where I had taken ballet, and if I could do a demonstration, that I took off my mouse ears, tail and ballet shoes: I said I was dressed up as a ball of dust. One of Peter's old friends from the boys' private school he attended came in a brown fur coat, he had silk pyjamas underneath, and played our organ while smoking a cigar, getting ashes all over the keys. He had a cruel habit of telling almost every girl he met that they looked like a male star he had seen in a film long ago – so and so, what's his name, the funny chap with the moustache, you're just the image, don't say are you related to...? Peter didn't say anything the time his friend compared me to a well-known silent film actor. He always took on a feigned look of inno-cence whenever anyone mentioned movies, as if he had spent his whole life in churches and libraries, though I had once overheard him humming *Singin' in the Rain* while in the bath.

The twins looked more and more like Peter. It made me howl and pull my hair, though it meant they would be handsome. Peter once told me I looked like an owl, my eyes were very round. His favourite Roman god was Minerva.

On my way to work I had to cross over a bridge, and I often imagined hanging the twins from it on ropes, their little legs kicking, saving them at the very last moment – I thought such an act would make me love them more. The image disturbed me so much, I saw it every time I passed over the bridge, so I took to running over it, arriving at work sweaty and full of pity for my children.

Peter sent a postcard to my mother's house, she called me to say there was a 'Spanish or Italian letter' waiting for me. It was written in Latin and he said he was faring well. It had an American stamp on it, though it was an antique postcard of broken columns at Pompeii. He didn't ask about the twins, with their heads that looked like shrunken, half-bald versions of his own. Though I didn't have his address, I went to a photo booth in a subway station with the intention of taking a family portrait. Perhaps I would send it to American newspapers. Inside the booth, the twins wouldn't stop screaming and struggling. They hadn't had their photos taken before.

In the photo Aeneas and Arthur weren't on my lap, as I had put them, but sitting on a black wolf whose eyes reflected the photographic flash. It had a horrible, fanged grin. I stuffed it in my pocket and pushed the stroller home, the twins were screaming, I had to belt them in.

After I got them to sleep, I took the photo out of my coat pocket and looked at it again. I didn't see why Aeneas and Arthur had cried so much. The wolf was handsome.

The longer I looked at the photograph, the larger it seemed, until I noticed the photograph was being held between two small black paws rather than hands. I was covered in fur the same colour as my hair – black. I was too frightened to look in a mirror so I filled a bowl with water, and looked at my face. I had a long black nose and my eyes were green, as they were when I was a human. I wasn't shocked, I didn't feel like I looked that different.

I looked at the photograph again: yes it was me, the photo booth had somehow known before I transformed. I felt an urge to go outside and went through the back-yard door. I ate some old apples in a rubbish bin, killed a rat and sniffed some puddles. I wandered from alley to alley, from quiet street to quiet street – I had never been in an alleyway at night-time before, it had the inhuman liveliness of a puppet show.

Every night the same thing happened. I would put the twins to bed, read a while then, yawning, at around 9, turn into a wolf. I would then turn back into a human sometime around 3 or 4, those hours of transformation were always blurry like my memory of *The Nutcracker*.

As a wolf, I had no fear of jumping through windows. I stole, from bookstores, grocery stores, clothing shops, even flower shops. I carried things home in my mouth – bouquets and novels and sausages.

I was back in human form by morning, though some-times I had stray black hairs on my chin or lips, my ears were a little long or a few of my nails were still dark and thick like claws – I told people they were damaged after being smushed under a window frame. I had a lot of small cuts from breaking windows – I told everyone the twins scratched me.

A few times, the twins were awake when I returned home from hunting and stealing. When I approached them, they crouched and covered their eyes although I had stolen them all sorts of expensive, fanciful toys. I had more breasts as a wolf, but they refused to feed from me.

It ended up in the newspapers: 'Wild dog breaks into shops'. A man had seen me leave a toyshop with an expensive Julius Caesar doll in my mouth. 'It was a dark and horrid beast,' he said to the newspaper. 'I bet it was looking for a real baby to eat.' I needed a disguise for getting around while in wolf form.

On a weekend, I went to a costume shop and purchased a nice pink rubber mask of a girl's face, stretchable enough to fit over my long wolf's nose, with yellow braids attached to it, a blue and white Alice in Wonderland dress, and a dainty pair of Victorian boots perfectly sized for my back wolf paws. I felt I could trust the girl who worked behind the counter at the costume shop. She looked somewhat wolf-like herself, with a long nose. She gave me the toy pistol for free, and indistinguishable, fluffy animal ears for the twins to wear, though they cried when I tried to put them on their heads. At home, I had a Red Riding Hood cloak someone had left at our costume party. It was made out of felt and had a copper clasp.

When no one was in sight, and I found a store I wanted to steal from, I took off my costume in a hidden spot, and jumped through the windows, taking what I needed. I was much greedier as a wolf. I decided to take care of the old woman in the old home Peter and I had lived in. I broke in through the back of the shop, but when I went to eat the woman, still in a bag behind the counter, the smell of embalming chemicals was so repulsive to me that I couldn't do it. She seemed to have shrunk. I thought it would be better to leave her there than bury her in a nearby park. Instead, I chased a fat raccoon I found rooting in a compost bin, then stole a bag of pomegranates from a fruit and vegetable store.

The next morning, when I woke up, the twins were nowhere to be found. Not in the cupboards, or the bath, or the rubbish bin. I ran up and down the street and the alley, my belly and breasts flapping like the sad wings of a fowl. They were gone. I must have eaten them in the late hours of being a wolf. Usually I remembered my wolf hours clearly, but I had no memory of making a meal of my children. Yet my stomach was stretched, as if I had eaten something large. I retched, but nothing bloody or hairy came out. I drank cupfuls of coffee, trying to digest them as quickly as possible so they would be out of my body. After I went to the bathroom I looked into the bowl to see if there were any bits in my excrement. I found a tiny white bone. It could have been from a pigeon – I loved pigeons while in wolf form.

I sold all of Arthur and Aeneas's things, which didn't amount to much, around forty dollars. I bought myself some books and a plaid skirt which was too small for me.

Maybe Peter had come while I was asleep and taken them away. The idea very much relieved me. I imagined him raising them somewhere along the coast of the Black Sea, speaking to them only in Latin and making them herd sheep. I called the day care and their doctor, explaining that I was moving to Rome with the children.

That night, I stole enough brie from a cheese shop to make it look like I had a fridge full of moons. I made myself a meal of brie cheese, pomegranates and raw pigeons. I started to write something I called *Memoirs of a Wolf*. I wrote in Latin first – Latin is the human language wolves know best – then translated it into English when

I was in human form again the next morning.

Sometimes Susan arrived at work with a few stray brown hairs around her mouth, or a spot of blood, but I didn't say anything and neither did she, and we stopped asking each other about our children.

THE GOTHIC SOCIETY

The first act of the Gothic Society was no more than a grotesque scribble, a heavy, ugly face drawn with charcoal on the walls of a concrete underpass that was quickly washed away.

Then someone found a stone griffon perched on the edge of a garbage bin, a leering wooden monk in a bathroom stall, a store window replaced with stained glass depicting a saint, a stretch of concrete sidewalk painted with suffering and comical beings.

Increasingly, their acts became more detailed and preposterous. A woman discovered that a bunch of her jewels had faces carved into them, someone else a gargoyle tattoo on their back, and a car was found with three stone kings sitting inside.

One morning, the residents of a glass building heard their alarms ring in the dark. From the outside, their building had changed overnight, into some sort of rectangular windowless cathedral, every inch covered in mouldings. The material wasn't stone – the whole building would've collapsed under a stone façade – but something similar to spray foam.

A construction company was called in to remove the gothic crust and free the residents. (Some of the workers took pieces home – a gargoyle face, a bird – to place in their gardens, only to have their gardens encrusted with gothic – every inch of green, every flower covered in nasty faces and snakes, fish, and virgins.) Some windows were broken during the procedure, and the next morning, the empty spaces were filled in with grey faces, vines and winged beings once more. The building had to be abandoned.

The Gothic Society was compared to zebra mussels,

to leprosy, to feral cats and urban foxes. Its members were never identified.

WAXY

My new bedroom was an old kitchen. One wall was taken up by dozens of small cupboards and drawers, a fridge, a black stove and a little brown sink with a beige hose hanging out of it like a child's leg. The landlord told me the fridge and stove didn't work, but they were good for storing clothes and other things. I could use the fridge as a wardrobe, she said.

It was on the fourth floor of a fat house covered in green tarpaper, and shared a hall and bathroom with another room, where a couple lived. Neither of our rooms had doors, only door frames. All the windows looking out onto the street were covered in dirty sheets, giving the impression from the outside that the house was nothing more than an empty shell with a giant's patchwork blanket hanging on the other side.

Along with the fridge and stove, my room had a table, a stack of flimsy chairs and a couch, which I was to use as a bed.

The kitchen cupboards were painted green and the walls were papered a reddish brown, with water spots and black mould here and there that reminded me of tinned meat that has been opened and forgotten. The sink water only ran cold.

I was very relieved. As soon as I moved in, I removed the sheet covering my small window, and washed the glass with vinegar.

.

A few days before, a girl from my Factory said she was leaving her place, since her Man had done well on an Exam and she could afford to move, and she told me I could take it. I was desperate to find a place and another Man, but when I went to look it was no more than a curtained-off section of a gloomy room shared with two other couples. One of the Men had brown teeth and kept licking his upper lip and leering at me as I was shown around the room. All four of them shared one filthy hotplate, and the windows were covered in long, thick, mouldy purple curtains. Damp Philosophy Books were stacked everywhere. In one corner there was a mountainous pile of empty tins, like a doll's house for vermin. The curled, hanging metal lids reminded me of the Man's protruding tongue.

There is nothing worse than being taken advantage of by someone else's Man. It's always considered the woman's fault. I knew I wouldn't be safe there. I was very fortunate to find the kitchen room through an advertisement posted in a café.

I had my own kerosene lamp, hotplate, toaster, tin bathtub and kettle, all of which Rollo let me keep because he assumed the next woman he lived with would have them too.

It was exciting to have a fridge in the room, even though it didn't work. When I opened it, it smelled like sour milk. I found a very withered fruit in one of its drawers, so wrinkled it almost looked like it had a face. I kept it on the windowsill as a kind of artistic curiosity until I realized it probably wasn't fruit but something much darker. I buried it in the small backyard of the house early one morning before any of the other lodgers were up.

The couple in the other room were named Pauline and Stuart. Pauline worked in a Factory sewing ladies' intimates. She brought home samples for herself and spent a lot of time modelling them in the bathroom, where the mirror was. Mirrors were extremely expensive, we were lucky to have one, but Pauline was such a bathroom hog I had to buy a chamber pot for my room. She was anorexic and so the lingerie just hung off her in a sad way. She kept the bathroom door open when examining herself in the mirror, I suppose she wanted Stuart to pass by and see her.

She rarely flushed the toilet after she used it. She left small dark pellets in the bowl, like rabbits' droppings.

.

I wasn't frightened of Stuart because he seemed very preoccupied with himself.

He spent his time at home pacing their room, with a Philosophy Book under his arm, smoking his pipe and listening to records by Wagner and Tchaikovsky. He tried to look like he was deep in thought, but I was sure the only thing on his mind was his next tinned meat sandwich. He had a meaty smell about him. Often my hotplate wouldn't work on account of Stuart hogging all the electricity for his records. I ruined a lot of eggs that way, and had to drink my coffee powder mixed with cold water.

Stuart wore a red quilted night-robe with rolled up corduroy trousers underneath, and velvet smoking slippers with a slight heel, and his red-blonde hair stuck up unbrushed and very dry. When he went out, to an Exam, or to buy tobacco and records, he changed his robe for an unwashed Oxford shirt and a green jumper with leather elbow patches.

He never brought much Exam money home. Often he returned slightly drunk, as it was a common custom for Men to go for a drink after one of their Exams, but I think Stuart pretended to be more drunk than he was so that Pauline would think he'd won a big Exam prize and spent it all on drink. Sometimes I don't even think he went to a bar – I couldn't smell any alcohol on him – but just walked around till evening before coming home.

'Next Time, Don't Spend Your Prize Money On Drink,' Pauline would say in a very loud, but not yelling, voice, as if speaking to a half-deaf person she wasn't cross at.

If one's Man did not do well on Exams, it was considered the woman's fault for not providing a nurturing enough environment in which they could excel.

·

I was jealous of Pauline's underthings. I didn't have anything I could bring home from my Factory, besides bits of sewing machine, but you couldn't do anything with them unless you had an iron frame, which was too large to pocket. It was my job to paint the name of the sewing machine company onto the frame, in gold paint: NIGHTINGALE.

When I first got the job, I felt bored and cruel painting NIGHTINGALE on all the machines. They looked like frightened black cats, and would all have the exact same name. I thought it would be so lovely to give one a name like DANCEY or VERONICA, but of course I would be fired. It didn't take long for it to feel like the only word I knew how to write was NIGHTINGALE.

In Pauline and Stuart's room, I could see women's underthings hanging everywhere in abundance like cobwebs, insects and flowers, but Pauline did not offer to give me any. Their room was papered muddy green. The most important thing they owned, besides a bed, a wardrobe, and Stuart's desk – all matching brown – was a gramophone, which loomed over everything else like a grand rotting flower.

I didn't have any nice underthings, perhaps Rollo wouldn't have left me if I'd had some. He and I parted ways after he won a large Exam prize. He wanted to find a nicer place to live and a prettier girl to take care of him. I wasn't too upset, I had prepared for something like this to happen, and I was proud he finally did so well on a big Exam.

When I first started dating him, I took him to the cinema. It was very expensive but I wanted to show Rollo I would not only take care of him but also show him a marvellous time. The film was called *A Virtuous Woman*. I didn't remember any of it, only the way the title was written in big letters on a black background. Whenever I closed my eyes, I saw the word NIGHTINGALE floating in black, like a film that was just beginning.

During the short time when I did not have a Man, I bought myself a grey trench coat, some plastic flowers, a pair of red rubber sandals, a tweed skirt with a few fixable moth holes and a third pair of dungarees, which I needed for work.

I felt good, but it was frowned upon to be Manless. I knew people would become suspicious of me if I went without one for too long. The way to meet Men was to go to a café, order a coffee and wait for a Man to talk to you. They often went, in groups, to cafés to study. The cafés had wooden booths and stools, and the floors and walls were all tiled. In the cheaper cafés the tiles were filthy and cracked, in more expensive ones they smelled strongly of bleach. The first question a Man always asked was what type of Factory you worked in. Ideal were the ones that disfigured a woman the least and paid the most.

41

Pauline's job was better than mine; she could've found a better Man than Stuart, though perhaps not because her anorexia was unappealing. Men really liked women to have breasts for them to fondle when they were nervous.

My hands were rather ruined from the chemicals in the paint I used at work. I thought about wearing gloves to the café, but that would've been deceitful, and if part of you that is normally shown is conspicuously covered, the Men know it is hiding some sort of disfigurement. I didn't want them to imagine my hands were worse than they actually were. I was lucky not to have a disfigured face, though I did have a nasty cough sometimes.

·

One day at a café I saw a tall, red-haired young Man with lots of freckles who appealed, but a girl with brown ringlets and a black eyepatch came in sobbing and pulled him out by the sleeve of his coat before we had a chance to talk.

I felt intolerably miserable. There were posters everywhere reminding me I was Manless:

TAKE CARE OF YOUR MAN
A GOOD LADY DOES NOT LET HER MAN LOITER
FEED YOUR MAN WELL

I traded a tin of meat with Pauline for a nice bra and panty set. I styled my hair into ringlets, it was a nice golden syrup colour, and used the lipstick I hadn't used since Rollo left me. I spent all my time off work sitting in cafés looking for Men. There was a couple I always saw: a thin, unshaven, greying, balding old Man wearing a filthy brown coat and a grimy chequered scarf, and a young woman with a nice prim body, nice hair and natural curls. She could have done much better if it weren't for her face: she was only sixteen or so, but her face had most likely been ruined by acid in a Factory. It wasn't the first time I'd seen something like it. They clung to each other in a desperate manner, and shared their food: one cup of coffee and a slice of toast cut in half and dribbled with golden syrup.

One evening I saw the Man sitting alone in the café. I assumed the girl had got pregnant and died. The Man only ordered a cup of coffee, and I didn't see him in the café for a few days after that – until he showed up with a new girl.

She was fat and bald with red splotches on her skull, and wore a fake-jewel necklace she played with repeatedly. The Man ordered a whole Golden Syrup Toast for himself and ate it greedily, chewing with his mouth wide open in a grin. I felt ill, and never went back to that café again. It didn't much matter, the café menus were the same everywhere:

COFFEE

GOLDEN SYRUP TOAST

BOILED TINNED MEAT WITH TOAST

The tinned meat became grey when it was boiled and made the toast all wet; most people just ordered Golden Syrup Toast with Coffee. There were also pubs, that sold beer and gin, but, like libraries, women weren't allowed in those. They were places for Men to socialize and study for their Exams in peace.

In a café I met a girl named Ann who played the electric Hammond organ in a Bar to entertain the Men, jolly songs to help them relax. She was bulky and had a downy moustache and very thick legs, I think from sitting at the organ all day long pressing the pedal. She smoked very quickly, bringing the cigarette to her mouth the way a greedy person eats little snacks.

She danced her fingers across the table, her shoulders wiggling along, making a buzzing with her mouth to demonstrate the organ sound.

She told me she used to have the most beautiful curls but had to cut them off because intoxicated Men would grab them. She now had a closely cropped bowl cut. She wore a blue dress with a plastic corsage safety-pinned to her chest and had sweat stains under her arms.

She was on her break: she wasn't allowed to eat in the Bar. They sold beer, gin, gherkins and toast. Gherkins were the special thing there. Sometimes she and the other girls snuck some gherkins home with them. A green thing was a fine thing to eat, so long as it wasn't mould, Ann said. Chop them up and put them in a sandwich with mushed boiled eggs and tinned meat. If your Man is worth anything, he'll bring you back a gherkin from the bar. I was too embarrassed to say I didn't have a Man.

Her Man was named Tiny Bernard, and she told me his hands were like chicken's feet, all bent with only three fingers and a little stump that was hardly a thumb. He was quite smart but never did well on Exams because he wrote so slowly. He could never finish before the time was up. Ann said she had fine hands aplenty and it was unfair they wouldn't let her assist him with writing Exams or give him an extra few hours.

Tiny Bernard was her first Man, and would be her last, she said. 'I wouldn't trade him for All the Golden Syrup in the World,' she told me before going back to work.

44

As she left, I noticed the seat of her dress was faded and brownish from sitting so much, and I was glad I got to wear dungarees to work instead of easily ruined dresses.

I stayed in the café until it was dark, and signs for Examinations were lit up all along the street. As I left, I noticed a young Man stood with his back pressed to the wall of the building across the street. Above him was a sign that said:

24 HOURS EXAMS WE PAY CASH

Between his legs was a child's suitcase with a white rabbit wearing a bonnet embroidered on the cover.

The young Man wore a long green woman's overcoat, a yellow jumper, wool trousers too wide and short for his long legs, and funny shoes with the laces missing. He was peeing without his trousers undone, the inner thigh of his left trouser leg quickly darkening. His hair was black, and very sparse, like the hair of a woman who works in a Factory full of chemicals. He looked about seventeen or so. I was taught not to judge a Man by his looks, that it was the inside that counts, but this one was so beautiful I wouldn't have cared if he were stuffed with straw. I couldn't wait for him to talk to me, he might never. I put my ugly hands in my pockets before I approached him, just in case.

The suitcase was a fortunate sign. Perhaps he had just left a woman and needed a new one, or perhaps even better, had never had one at all. He seemed very intoxicated, or nervous from Exams, and agreed to come home with me immediately. I would take care of him, I said, and carried his suitcase for him back to my house.

I didn't realize how bad he smelled until we were in

the hall of my building, a mixture of urine, rotten milk and mice.

There wasn't enough electricity for hot water, so he had to take a quick cold bath. I scrubbed him furiously with soap until he was red and shivering.

I gave him a baggy blue jumper with brass buttons, a white cotton nightie to wear and a cup of hot beef-flavoured broth and toast, as he was so cold from the bath. He also put on grey socks and grey underwear from his suitcase, but I made him take them off because they smelled mildewy from not being dried properly. I lent him a pair of my own socks. As he ate, I unpacked the rest of his things: some children's books and clothes.

When I saw he had no Philosophy Books, I realized he probably didn't have any identification papers either. I was frightened, but I had already brought him home.

When he heard Pauline and Stuart come up the stairs and enter the room across the foyer he got frightened and tried to leave. I pushed him onto my couch and held him down, putting one of my hands across his mouth. 'They were expecting me to get a Man any day now. They don't need to know you don't have papers.'

He was skinny enough that we could both fit comfortably on my saggy couch. It was like lying next to a beautiful, pale branch. I was terrified that he would leave me as soon as I fell asleep, but when I woke in the middle of the night it was only because he was trying to enter me, so I spread my legs to make it easier for him.

His name was Paul and he was no one and had never done an Exam.

When he was born his parents called him Bluey because he was blue and cold. Growing up, he had slept beside the open oven door.

Once they put him in the oven, promising they

wouldn't turn it on, and told him not to come out until it was quiet. When he came out, the apartment was empty and his parents were gone. Some older women took him in until it was no longer safe, he was illegal, and they didn't want anyone thinking he was their child. He lived under stairs, in shadows, cupboards and attics.

He gave himself the name Paul, from a children's book, because the name Bluey reminded him too much of his parents and made him sad. He was missing many teeth and sometimes couldn't control his bladder. I didn't mind because one of the first things a girl learns in school is that every Man has his own special problems, and it's one's duty to take care of them. I became used to cleaning, and also to the sight of Paul's saggy grey underpants draped over every surface of our room, dripping like rainclouds as they dried. After his first night living with me, I was so worried about leaving him alone, I painted the word 'nightingale' wrong on three sewing machines, though it was the word I knew best in the world.

'NITINGALE, NIGTINGALE, NIGHTNGALE.'

When I came home, Stuart was in our kitchen, walking back and forth, talking to Paul who sat demurely on a fold-out chair, his face very pale, his knees pressed together. He was nodding and nodding, Stuart was talking about Exams, and to my relief, not asking Paul any questions.

I told Stuart it was time to go, that Paul needed his dinner.

Paul said Stuart went on and on about Exams and Paul didn't know a single thing he was talking about.

The next morning I left Paul some money to go sit in cafés and go to the flea market. I bought him some Philosophy Books so Pauline and Stuart wouldn't get suspicious.

For a while Stuart thought Paul was some sort of young genius because he was so vague, but soon forgot about him when he realized Paul was of no direct use to him.

As he wasn't registered for Exams, Paul spent his time wandering or making our home better. He made a couple of rag rugs to cover our cold floor, was good at darning clothes and knew how to cook eggs in all sorts of interesting ways. He nailed a wool blanket across our door frame so we could have more privacy. Sometimes we could see motion on the other side, as if someone was lightly punching the blanket, but didn't know if it was Pauline or Stuart.

Paul discovered that a few of our kitchen drawers were full of forks and spoons.

Only a fool would leave so many spoons and forks in a place like this and not expect them to be stolen, he said. Perhaps they were left by the last person, and the landlord was too lazy to look through the apartment for treasures before renting it out again. After what I found in the fridge, I had been too frightened to open any of the cupboards.

He sold some of the forks and spoons at a flea market and came back with a sack of yellow onions. For weeks we ate fried onions with bread. The smell drove Pauline crazy. What she did eat was as unflavoured as possible: glasses of ration milk and slices of apple.

We also splurged on a sweet bun to share, sold from the same bakery where I bought bread, but the bits of red and green candied fruit stuck on top were actually bits of plastic, and Paul almost choked on one. He cried for a long time after.

From my Factory I got rations of powdered milk,

eggs, margarine, tinned meat, tinned peaches, a fresh, waxed apple, beef-flavoured bouillon cubes and a small pouch of low-grade tobacco. Every month one was given a small circle of pale yellow cheese with an orange-coloured rind. Many said it didn't melt, but just kind of sweated. I enjoyed it all the same, especially eaten with the tinned peaches. We were also given a tin of golden syrup quarterly.

During the time between Rollo and Paul, instead of saving the non-perishable items as a woman was supposed to when single, I ate all the food myself and put on weight.

The rest of our earnings were meant for rent, bread and tobacco – if one's Man did not have any prize money from Exams to spend on it – along with Philosophy Books and any other needs a Man might have. Paul didn't use tobacco, and didn't have many needs. He didn't even eat as much as me.

My only worry, besides Pauline and Stuart discovering Paul wasn't registered for Exams, was having a baby. Paul taught me all sorts of Uncommon tricks I had never tried before that were nice, and according to him didn't cause babies.

It would take several months of saving my salary without buying anything to be able to afford contraceptives. It was near impossible without Exam prize money. Some Men didn't like to spend their prize money on contraceptives; they preferred alcohol, tobacco and bowties. There were always stories about girls who died or were left disabled by jumping down stairs to terminate a pregnancy, or little blue babies left in rubbish bins or killed in ovens and sinks.

'He'll pay for it, I know he will, he loves me,' a lot of them said, but of course, that rarely happened and the girl died some way or another. It was more affordable just to find a new woman. To register a pregnancy and birth was even more expensive than contraceptives, and I could afford neither without Exam money.

It was possible for some people though, that's how there were so many Men and women, me included. To find a Man who had enough Exam prize money and also wanted to have children, that was the Goal of Life. I don't remember my own parents. Boys and girls were taken away from home at age three. Girls were given five years of schooling in Life Skills and Prospects, then went to work in a Training Factory, which usually made boys' clothes and toys, while boys stayed in school until sixteen when they started Examinations and began looking for a woman to care for them.

It was common for boys to begin with an older woman, one who was no longer fertile and so couldn't get them into trouble, while they learnt how to get relaxation and pleasure from women. Of course, the older women, despite those advantages, had competition from women my age, in their mid-twenties, who were more sexually appealing and desperate to get as young a Man as possible because there was more hope of them succeeding compared to the older Men. The odd, idiot girl became attached to an older Man, who was obviously a failure at Exams and Life. These types of couples were the laughing stock of Society.

Women stayed in Training Factory dormitories, where bed and board was covered, until around the age of thirteen. During that time we were given a small wage that we were supposed to eventually spend on things to make our home and ourselves appeal to Men – stockings or a kettle, for example. We were told that if you brought a Man home and didn't have a kettle or toilet paper, he would laugh at you and leave. They were used to the comforts of their school dormitories. We left the dorm with enough money to rent a room and a suitcase full of practical things, ready to start looking for Men and find better jobs.

When a woman first got out of the Training Factory dorms, the Men went crazy for her, especially if she hadn't started menstruating. Usually they already lived with a woman who knew how to take care of them, and just wanted to use you. One could only learn so much from School and Books about Men, so it was considered good experience to learn what sort of Men were out there and what they liked, as long as you didn't get pregnant or a disease. Some girls didn't make it through their first year out of dormitories. I still became sad when I thought about the friends I had lost that way. After my first, I never went with any Man who didn't have birth control, that's how I survived. I met Rollo a few years after leaving dormitories, he was in his twenties and wise about birth control and sacrificed lots of nice things in order for me to have it, like higher grade tobacco and records.

Girls who hadn't started to menstruate were called Cheaps, because they didn't require birth control. There were some Men who hung around the factory dormitories looking for Cheaps. Many girls, myself included, slept with those Men so we could learn, and wouldn't make fools of ourselves when we went out on our own to meet better Men to live with. Once in a while a girl died from the pain, so you had to be careful and not be too young or careless. It could also cause Nightmares, and a Man did not want to settle down with a girl who had Nightmares or was nervous.

Men liked stability and ease most of all, but still,

there were those who only went for Cheaps and ruined lots of them.

.

I continued to gain weight and blamed it on Paul's small appetite, until my periods stopped. Pauline didn't get a period on account of her anorexia. I started to wear jumpers over my dungarees to work, hoping no one would notice.

There wasn't even a chance of registering our baby because Paul had no papers. There was something liberating in that, though the thought of pain and maybe even dying scared me. There would be no one to take care of Paul, and he had become so used to having a regular home.

Our neighbourhood wasn't well-off, so you didn't see babies there, besides the dead ones in bins or wrapped up in cloth along the pavement. One weekend, in the early stages of my pregnancy, I took a tram to a better-off neighbourhood, where successful Men lived, to try to see some Mothers. And I did, pushing prams. They looked cautious, tired and blissful. I tried to peek into their prams to see a real, live baby, but I was shy. I could hear some of them crying and wondered how I could stop mine from making so much noise when it arrived.

The women had nice make-up, faces and clothes and, despite all the frightening trials ahead of me, I felt a mysterious excitement. They would have to give their children away aged three, but as long as I kept my child hidden, and alive, it was mine to keep.

The flea markets had all sorts of plastic dollies, carriages and colourful alphabet blocks but we were too afraid someone would notice us buying baby things and report us. Paul made a rubber-band ball, covered it with glue so no bands would become loose and swallowed by our child, and painted a red star on it.

He also sewed some wonderful dolls using old socks with colourful yarn from old jumpers for the hair, and drew cheery faces on them.

.

I gave birth on a Friday, after work. I had felt cramped and dizzy all day, and my NIGHTINGALES were all shaky. When I got home, I ate four boiled eggs, which made me feel worse, and a few hours later went to the bathroom where I had diarrhoea and gave birth at the same time. I stuffed toilet paper in my mouth and chewed on it so I wouldn't scream. I wrapped the little thing, no bigger than a hand, up in paper and ran back into the kitchen to wash it with warmed up water from the kettle and disinfectant.

It was a tiny, waxy child, like a little cheese rind, that barely ever cried. I think it knew by some survival instinct it wasn't supposed to, and Paul was very attentive, feeding it milk and changing its rag diapers before it became upset. He was good with children, perhaps from reading so many children's books.

We were too scared to name it properly so we just called it Waxy.

We decided that when our child was old and wise enough to choose its own real name, it could have one.

Waxy was so small, I thought at first that giving birth wasn't much different from menstruating, but then I fainted the Monday back at work. They gave me the afternoon off and an extra ration of beef-flavoured bouillon, assuming I was anaemic. My afternoon off was bliss, I lay on our couch with Waxy tucked underneath my nightie, and Paul read us all his books, one after the other.

We left Waxy's cord on until it became all brown and wilted and fell off. I flushed it down the toilet.

Paul wanted to use the fridge as a hidden nursery for Waxy, but I was too scared of Waxy suffocating. We found an old picnic basket at the flea market that had a lid with lots of holes in it. We put a doll and pillow inside, and Waxy seemed to like it all right. We hid the basket behind a large framed picture of an old Man with a beard, also from the flea market.

Paul went on long walks with Waxy bundled under his coat in a scarf, but I wouldn't let him take Waxy to flea markets because of all the animals.

Women there sold toads, worms, and chickens that looked diseased, without many feathers. I knew someone who had died from buying one of those chickens and eating it; it was safest to eat meat from one's Factory rations. Some people boiled and fried the toads. One could also find rats, pigeons, rabbits. You were a desperate woman if you were trying to sell those, but some people were stupid enough to buy them, especially baby rabbits.

.

I knew a girl who stuck an all-white pigeon feather in her hair because she thought it was rare and beautiful, but the feather was full of diseases and she went blind. Another girl bought a baby rabbit as a pet, but it bit her and she died horribly.

There were women all around whose job it was to

spray poison on wild animals; they had the worst skin and the thinnest hair. Very few of them had Men.

Once, Paul came home from one of his walks with an old cracker tin with a picture of a boy in a green jumper feeding jam-covered crackers to a hound dog. The tin was rectangular-shaped, house-like, and Paul kept going on about how wonderful it would be if it were house-sized and we could live inside happily ever after, with the hound dog to watch over us, and nice white crackers to eat.

The tin would get really hot and burn us, I told him, and it would be dark without windows. He became quiet, but soon seemed to forget about the tin. I used it to protect our coffee powder from vermin, but kept finding buttons, rolled-up bits of paper and small plastic flowers inside.

I asked Paul about it and he told me that once someone gave him a slice of ginger-powder cake with a penny hidden inside and it was the best thing that ever happened to him before he met me. He thought it brought good luck and wouldn't listen when I told him I could choke on one of the buttons.

When Waxy had wind, it opened its mouth in a strange silent howl. Paul covered one of his fingers in golden syrup and stuck it in the baby's mouth to suck on like a soother, but one day it didn't work and Waxy let out a horrible howl, its first one, the one it didn't make when it was born, and I felt both elated it had made such a sound, and terribly frightened the neighbours would hear. Stuart did.

He pushed back our wool door and barged into our kitchen with his pipe in his mouth. He stared at Waxy, whom Paul was holding.

'Pauline's tobacco isn't enough for me and her,' he

said, and took my tobacco tin off our table, leaving our kitchen without another look at Waxy.

Neither of us could sleep that night, Paul kept mumbling on about the cracker tin again, but Stuart didn't report us the next day, nor did Pauline seem to know about our little one. However, on ration day, Stuart came into our kitchen and took my tobacco again, along with a tin of meat. After a couple of weeks he told us there was much better tobacco available in the world, like Goodes' tobacco, for example, and we knew the Factory ration tobacco was no longer enough to keep him quiet. It really ate into our budget. Paul sold more forks and spoons, but we still couldn't afford to buy bread anymore. We had to eat our eggs and meat without toast, and soon our eggs without meat. Stuart ate all of Pauline's and our tinned meat. He came into our kitchen whenever he pleased to help himself to our coffee and margarine, though he had enough in his own room, and his meaty smell was unbearable.

.

Then Stuart became Sick.

They did not have enough money for medicine. Pauline blackmailed us into giving it to them. Paul and I had to sell all of our chairs and most of my clothes, including my red sandals and also some of Paul's books. Being Sick without savings was foolish – every responsible person put away a bit of money from their Exams and jobs into a Sick savings pot – even I had, and used it to buy a small bottle of disinfectant for having Waxy.

They refused to sell their gramophone at the market, and Stuart kept it on all the time while he lay in bed and it used our entire ration of electricity. Pauline rubbed Stuart with disinfectant and gave him a terrible-smelling green syrup and little white vitamins but none of it helped and she threw the medicine away.

Taking out the garbage a couple of days after Stuart's illness started, I noticed the meat tins piled up on our hall were punctured with tiny holes, they looked like little cages.

I didn't know whether it was Pauline or Paul that did it. Paul seemed too innocent, and Pauline really did love Stuart.

She sat at his bedside, feeding him cups of plain boiled water, and wearing a blue scarf over her head, like in the picture she had of a woman wearing a red and blue coat surrounded by glitter and other nice things.

Pauline asked Paul to take Stuart water during the day when Pauline was at work, but I was never sure Paul did. He was so terrified of Waxy catching the Sickness that he kept our window open for fresh air, and spent as much time as possible outside, with a few boiled eggs and a thermos of coffee in a knapsack, Waxy deep beneath his coat. There was always a huge, nasty mess for Pauline to clean when she got home from work, Stuart could never make it to the bathroom and most of the time could not keep food down. All he wanted to eat was tinned peaches and apples, Pauline made us give them ours and I was terribly worried about Paul not getting enough vitamin C, though the smell of thrown-up tinned peaches in the hall made Paul swear he would never eat them again.

·

Of course, Pauline couldn't quit work, and Stuart died while she was away. She came home and he was all putrid and still. Two heavyset women wearing old baggy men's suits came to take the body away. It cost an enormous amount and I had to pay for it. They gave Pauline harsh looks for allowing her Man to get Sick and die. One of the women was pockmarked, and both of them wore their hair in buns, one of them had brown powder in her hair, to make it look thicker than it was. I suppose there were lots of chemicals in their line of work and it ruined their hair and skin. Their shoes were heavy going down the steps, and Stuart's body, wrapped in a green wool blanket, was terribly swollen.

The night after they took Stuart away I had a dream he was still alive, but his legs were made out of tinned meat. He said they were too fat and made me chew on them until they were thin and graceful, but still an awful red in colour, and terribly dry-tasting. I woke up with a headache from dehydration, and Waxy, who was sleeping in a small crevice between us, had a filthy nappy. Poor Waxy's little legs were skinny and pasty like Paul's fingers. I kissed them and wept as I changed Waxy's nappy on the kitchen table.

.

Pauline had the gramophone and lots of lingerie so she would have no trouble finding a new Man, but weeks went by without her bringing one home.

Since she rarely ate, she had a stockpile of tinned meat, tobacco, and other goods which she placed around Stuart's gramophone, I think as a memorial. The eggs and apples rotted, it smelled horrible passing her room. Around the house she took to wearing Stuart's old robe, her lingerie underneath, and a navy blue tam-o'-shanter. She lurked in the stairwell like a spider, and sometimes pawed at our wool door, asking for odd things, such as buttons, forks, and socks. She didn't take any interest in Waxy, but we said yes to everything she asked, it was too dangerous for us to move anywhere else.

We couldn't say no when she stuck her head through the side of our wool door and said in a loud whisper, 'I've seen and heard you do Uncommon things to her, Paul, I want you to do them to me, or I'll report you.'

She came into our kitchen wearing nothing underneath Stuart's robe, which was turning all ratty, and I could see she was completely hairless. It made me think of an awful mixture of things: maggots, babies, eggs and old bread. 'A Man registered for Exams wouldn't know how to do things like that,' she said. She took Paul by the hand and pulled him out. Waxy cried. So did I, once they were both out of the kitchen. When he came back he said it was like trying to eat cold worms. He drank five cups of coffee and kept trying to pick at Waxy's cradle cap. Pauline asked him to do it almost every day. Paul wet our couch more frequently, and I woke up all the time sweaty from bad dreams.

I had a nightmare that Paul had NIGHTINGALE written on his back and I couldn't scrub it off no matter how hard I tried. The next morning, I had to look all over his body to find it but I couldn't.

Paul doing things to Pauline would stop her from finding a new Man who would possibly report us, but I couldn't stand how it made Paul feel.

·

One morning, before work, I went into the bathroom and discovered

PAULINE + PAUL

carved into the door frame.

I was very upset, so upset that Paul said he would change his name. He looked through his books and read all the names aloud:

'George.'

'Billy.'

'Rupert.'

'Cyril.'

But none of them was quite right.

His name was stuck to him like a tattoo. I liked the name Paul. If only there weren't Paulines in the world. They were both thin with thin black hair, as if they had been made in the same Factory. If Paul, Waxy and I just got up and left she would report us, and we would be chased. We really started to hate our home, we felt trapped inside. Paul said it was like living in the belly of a toad, and that Pauline was like a nasty tongue that licked everything so it smelled like her. She demanded more and more time with Paul, he had to spend his whole evenings and nights with her. It gave Waxy colic; I had to bang pots and sing so the other neighbours wouldn't hear the crying. I didn't get any sleep and got in trouble at work for writing NIGHT, NIGHT, NIGHT, NIGHT on four sewing machines, forgetting the rest of the word.

Paul acted morose around her, he just stood or sat and sulked when he wasn't making love to her in Uncommon ways, but Pauline acted horribly silly, laughing and playfully slapping him and putting bits of golden syrup on her face with a spoon which she made Paul kiss off.

We needed to make her even with us. If she had a baby too, she couldn't report ours, Paul decided. Then we could run away and live the type of Life he had had before, lurking and hiding but free of Pauline, who would hopefully throw herself down the stairs or out of the window if she didn't die from birth or shame.

I told him it was impossible, Pauline couldn't have babies because she was too thin. Paul said we just have to fatten her up like the witches do to children in the fairy tales he used to read to me when we had more time together.

Paul started to have sex with her in the common manner, he was able to make her want to do it with him by being less morose and giggling along with her sometimes. He didn't mind doing it the common way as he did doing Uncommon tricks, because it was to hurt Pauline in the end.

Having sex the common way made Pauline feel sentimental, I think. She started to eat a little more, but it wasn't enough. One weekend morning, I stood in the bathroom with my dungarees pulled down, examining my breasts in the mirror. They were all swollen with milk, and Paul stood watching me and fondling himself just as Pauline came upstairs. We had planned it out that way.

He convinced her to eat bread soaked in milk, tinned peach juice and golden syrup, boiled eggs and coffee with milk, often bringing it to her while she was naked in bed. She started to grow. The new fat did not look very nice on her. Her hair didn't get any thicker. I thought she looked like a sweet bun with hairs and pigeons' eyeballs stuck to it. She started to fill out her lingerie, and Paul tried to act very enthusiastic and In Love, but when he was lying beside me on our couch he would say in a flat voice, 'I hate her, I hate her,' until he got so riled up he had to walk in circles around our kitchen, clapping his hands, until it was time for me to go to work.

·

We both felt better the day she came home from work with a blood stain on the seat of her dungarees that she was unaware of. When she got undressed, she screamed and said Paul was trying to murder her. She ran around with blood dribbling down her thighs and on her hands, Paul had to clean it off her then placate her in bed with sweet songs and kisses.

She told Paul she could no longer do it the common way with him, because she didn't want to have a You-Know-What. Paul and I decided we would have to make her pregnant whether she liked it or not. One evening, Paul put one of Stuart's old Tchaikovsky records on, a rather nice waltz, so the neighbours wouldn't hear when he went up behind her, grabbed her neck and pushed her onto her bedroom floor, forcing himself inside her. After, he held her feet and made her do a headstand so all the stuff he put inside her would trickle deep down inside her like golden syrup.

I told him to do it twice, just in case. He hit her until she was unconscious and did it a third time while I packed up the things we needed. He put a blanket over her head in case she woke up and saw us leaving. We put Waxy in a carpetbag, and floppy hats on our heads, and crept down the stairs of the house like ants carrying crumbs. We walked in no particular direction, avoiding the bright and flashing Exam signs, Men smoking and arguing underneath them, crumpled notepaper between their fists.

As it became colder, we went into an alley, took Waxy out of the carpetbag, and put the little thing under Paul's coat. We longed to stop for a coffee somewhere, but we were too afraid. Paul and I put socks on our hands to keep them warm, since we didn't own mittens. They made us look fingerless, like Paul's homemade dolls.

He started to go on again about the cracker tin, which was tied to his back with string since it didn't fit in his suitcase. My knapsack sagged with home-made nappies, tins of fruit and extra jumpers.

'We just need to find a safe place to put it down so we can live in it,' Paul repeated every few minutes.

'I told you before, Paul, it's too small.'

'You never know what may happen,' he said in a very grand, serious voice, and I was too tired to contradict him anymore. I could smell Waxy underneath his coat, like a rancid molar in the back of one's mouth.

We walked and walked, and as the sun came out, the regular time I went to work, I knew I would never paint the word NIGHTINGALE again. So I said it out loud again and again until things felt calm, nice and sure.

'Night-in-gale, Night-in-gale, Night-in-gale.'

THE DOLL'S ALPHABET

The Doll's Alphabet has eleven letters:

A B C D I L M N O P U

THE MERMAID

She wasn't like known mermaids, divided in two, fish bottom, a lady on top. The fish and the human were blended together like tea with milk. She had greyish skin, pale blonde hair, fish mouth and eyes – the eyes behind round ship window glasses, the stooped look of a jumping dolphin, and hardly any chin at all. She often wore a blue wool coat, a string of pearls, and green galoshes without any shoes underneath.

The village was only two miles from the sea, the air was salty, once a seal wandered into town. The mermaid must have done the same.

The mermaid loved silver things, Evelyn saw her take a piece of tinfoil out of a rubbish bin, roll it into a ball and stick it in her purse. My brother might fancy a mermaid, thought Evelyn. Vyvyan didn't have any interests or activities – a mermaid just might be the thing.

Evelyn owned a shop called Old Time Things that had belonged to their father. It was on the first floor of a Tudor house and sold clocks, books, furniture, jewellery, mirrors, dolls, crockery, even coins and witch bottles he found on the beach.

Evelyn washed the window and filled it with silver things, teapots, earrings, chains, boxes, candlesticks, urns, forks, knives. It drew the mermaid in. He hid behind a grandfather clock, holding a green rug. As she reached for a silver fork, he jumped out, wrapped her up and took her upstairs. His brother lived on the third floor, he was too tall for the attic. Evelyn and his wife Emmeline used the attic as their bedroom.

'What have you there?' said Emmeline, looking up from her Homer. She read on the stairs, using a stained glass lamp on a long brown crowd. It gave her a ghoulish blue and green look.

'A thing for Vyvyan,' said Evelyn.

Everyday, Evelyn brought his brother a pot of very dark tea and a fish sandwich with the head and tail sticking out. He wouldn't eat anything else. He did not have a bed, he wouldn't sleep in one, but sometimes suffered a blanket on his knees in winter.

Their father was as tall as Vyvyan, but brilliant in mind, and had opened the shop. There was a hole in the shop ceiling so he could stand comfortably, now covered with a cloth. When he died the funeral parlour wanted to charge them for two coffins, and the cemetery for two grave plots, so Evelyn sold his body to a scientist in London, asking if they could just keep one piece to bury – a finger – which the scientist obliged them. The finger was so long they buried it in a child's coffin using the money from the scientist.

Evelyn was five feet tall, he wore nice suits and shoes with a little heel on them to make him appear five feet something.

When he reached the third floor, Evelyn unfurled the carpet and the mermaid rolled out. Her glasses had fallen off. She put them back on, dusted herself off and stood up. Vyvyan ignored her. As well as being tall, he was very large-boned but thin, so his brow, wrists, chin, nose and shoulders all looked very prominent. He wore a suit, the same top hat since the age of seven, and had a unibrow. Once Evelyn tried to trim it because Emmeline had read somewhere that unibrows were evil, and Vyvyan had hit him so hard Evelyn flew across the room.

Evelyn left the room, locking the door behind him.

When he went to check on them later, the mermaid was standing in a dark corner, holding her purse in front of her. Vyvyan was still looking out of the window, his hands on his knees.

The next morning, along with Vyvyan's meal, he brought the mermaid a cup of tea, a tin of seaweed and a jar of salt.

That evening, looking up from their dinner of pork and brussels sprouts, Evelyn and Emmeline saw the mermaid standing in the kitchen door, smiling weakly and wringing her hands, her purse swinging on her arms.

'I suppose we can give her some pork,' said Evelyn, 'though I don't like that she's left my brother alone.'

After eating, the mermaid licked her silver knife and fork, she would have eaten them if Emmeline hadn't taken them away.

Emmeline, who wore clear plastic cat-eye glasses, didn't like other women who also wore glasses. While Evelyn served them tea and vanilla pudding for dessert, Emmeline opened a book by Thomas Carlyle and read, clearing her throat now and then.

Emmeline was raised by her father, and was the only person in town smart enough to go to university. Since she was young, she admired Evelyn from afar. He was dainty and wise looking. When she was brave enough, and had extra money, she would go into the shop, as it was the only place in town that sold books, very old ones mostly, but that was what Emmeline was interested in.

Often, in her schoolgirl days, she would sit in the bakery across from Old Time Things and watch Evelyn with a pair of brass binoculars while eating iced buns. The window of Old Time Things was so dusty it was hard to see in, but every now and then Evelyn stepped out of the shop to have a cigarette, he followed his father's rule of no smoking in the shop.

She wrote him a love note:

We are the only two people in town who wear glasses.

But it wasn't true. In their town, there was a twelve-year-old boy who wore glasses and an old woman with red frames, and a middle-aged man with a pince-nez. There was even a store that sold glasses.

She threw the note into the sea. When she was accepted into the most prestigious university in the country, she decided to tell Evelyn she loved him. She tucked her university acceptance letter into her bosom under her cardigan and went into Old Time Things.

If he said no, she would get on the train north and go to the university to study Ancient Greek for the rest of her life. She sat down on a footstool and said to Evelyn 'Will you be my sweetheart? I want to live here.'

Instead of going to university, she married Evelyn. He wasn't the promiscuous Ares she had imagined him to be. She didn't help out in the shop, and took no interest in Vyvyan. She spent all her time reading on the stairs between the first and second floor.

She hadn't had a baby yet; an ear-like thing once came out of her, and she put it in a box to keep in case more bits came out and she had to assemble them. She would name the child Priam or Zeus, though she didn't think she would have time to take care of it.

That night, when she and Evelyn were kissing in bed, their glasses on the nightstand, Emmeline saw the fuzzy outline of the mermaid standing in their bedroom door, her hands clasped together.

'Go back downstairs,' Emmeline growled, and the mermaid did.

Though Evelyn locked Vyvyan's door whenever he left the mermaid inside, she was always found somewhere else in the house: standing in the bathtub, sitting behind Emmeline on the stairs, licking silver plates in the shop, putting kitchen spoons and tin can lids in her purse.

'No more,' said Emmeline.

They took the mermaid on a train to a beach town twenty minutes away, luring her with a silver rattle.

The mermaid wandered down the beach, her eye caught something silver and glistening, and she leaned down to pick it up. Out of her view, Evelyn and Emmeline ran back to the train station, their hands against their faces, holding their glasses in place.

AGATA'S MACHINE

Agata and I were both eleven years old when she first introduced me to her machine. We were in all the same classes. She was sallow and thin, with enormous hands and feet. She wore her dark brown hair in a short bob, held back from her face with a plain, plastic barrette. Her eyebrows weren't thick, but they were long, stretching to her temples. Her mouth was wide, but her lips were thin, with an expressiveness that reminded me of worms.

She wasn't tormented by our schoolmates and teachers, as I was. The only student they treated worse than me was Large Barbara, who was so fat she walked with a cane, had one lazy eyeball, and a wart on her chin so long and thin it mocked the rest of her body. Agata wasn't teased or tormented because she was a genius. She excelled in the sciences and maths, and could write beautiful, complex poems, though she only did so when it was a school assignment. She often yawned and shook one of her legs in class; she finished her work before everyone else. Some teachers let her read her own books, imported ones in foreign languages, full of complicated diagrams just as mysterious to the rest of us as the words.

Though she wasn't bullied, she also didn't have any friends. She seemed above such trivialities. No one invited her to parties – it was impossible to imagine her at them. She spent her lunch break reading. She didn't play or gossip. She saw the other students as a nuisance, like flies or fleas. Some tried to pay her to do their homework, but she responded with, 'You think I don't have better things to do?' in a tone of voice that was arrogant, and delighted in its own arrogance, her worm mouth wiggling.

Agata's parents were poor because they had so many children, but they still bought her whatever she needed or desired so she could focus on her schoolwork: books, expensive pens, cigarettes. Agata was the eldest and the most promising of her siblings. The rest were snivelly, slow readers who wore second-hand clothes that had seen too many threadbare childhoods. Because their clothes were so old, so outdated, their hair so sparse, their limbs so rickety, and their foreheads so large, they looked like little old men, even the girls. Agata didn't care about clothes. I was sure her parents would buy her nice outfits, if she asked.

She wore cheap-looking floral dresses, meant for an older housewife, and large men's shoes – hand-me-downs from her father. When it was wet outside, she wore black rubber galoshes over her shoes, making her feet look even larger. In class she wore slippers of fuzzy grey wool.

I was vain and wore the same thin, white, feminine shoes all year round, even though the soles suffered under the pressure of my weight, and the material let water soak through, my toes and heels stained from the dye in my stockings. In class, I discreetly took my shoes off under my desk to let my feet dry, blue and black imprints on the inner lining of my shoes. These stains horrified and embarrassed me, as if the dye had come out of my body instead of my stockings.

One morning it was so wet outside that dyed water dripped from my feet onto the classroom floor. Agata, who was sitting behind me, whispered, 'Your foot is crying.'

She didn't say it loud enough for anyone else to hear, but I blushed.

Swiftly, she moved her own foot under my desk, and within a second the small puddle was gone.

She did it again and again, whenever a puddle formed, until my stockings, dry enough near the end of the day, ceased to drip.

Leaving class after school, she put her large hand on my arm and whispered in my ear. 'Come home with me, there's something I want to show you.'

I was filled with dread, as if a few more hours of class had been added to my day. What was she going to show me? Maths textbooks, a home laboratory kit? I was too afraid to say no, in case she would tell the rest of our class about my 'crying foot', in case she would yell, loud enough for everyone to hear, 'Your foot cries!'

I was unsure whether I was embarrassed walking home with her or not. I didn't like the disgusting sound of her galoshes, the smell of her cigarettes, but she walked with such ease and confidence, with such disdain for everyone we passed by in our village. She wore fingerless gloves, a canvas knapsack so full it sagged down her legs, and a ragged blue military coat with flaking gold buttons.

.

Agata's family lived on the main floor of a five-floor building. The landlord allowed Agata to use the attic as a study. In exchange, Agata's father cleaned and maintained the foyer and the halls of the building, though he already had a full-time job as a clerk at a small glassware factory that specialized in vases.

Her mother, with all her other children, was too busy to clean the halls herself, said Agata. We briefly stopped in the family apartment before heading to her attic.

There were children everywhere, and no sign of the life Agata lived; no books, only tacky lithographic prints of historic buildings, dark Madonna and Child icons dotting the walls like speckles on a crow's egg. I wondered if Agata had to share a bedroom with her siblings.

Her mother was thin and going bald. Her pregnant stomach was ridiculous and reminded me of a hard-boiled egg, a food no one at school would eat without shame because of its terrible smell and uncanny, wobbly movements once the shell was removed. She wore a cheap metal necklace, childish rings, and a dress just like Agata's. When introduced to her, I suppressed a giggle.

Agata didn't greet any of her younger siblings, but grabbed two bread rolls off the table.

'Bring us coffee in a bit,' she said to her mother, and pulled me out and upwards to her attic.

She unlocked the door with a key kept in one of her coat pockets, and took off her galoshes and shoes. She put on a pair of crusty-looking slippers from a ragged mat in the hall. I also took off my shoes, but the floor of her attic was dirty, covered with peeling linoleum, carpet and patches of wood, a repulsive mixture that reminded me of bandages that needed to be changed and the flaky, scabby skin underneath.

The walls of Agata's attic were half-covered in maps and diagrams, a large poster of the periodic table, a map of the world. There were books everywhere, telescopes, glass vials and microscopes. A green metal desk with a ragged, greasy armchair in front of it. A glass vase full of brown water and cigarette butts. Socks, papers, teacups and mousetraps – one with a flattened and dried mouse under its metal bar. I had assumed she would be meticulous and clean.

In the middle of the attic was something large and awkwardly shaped covered with a wool blanket. In one corner there was a headless garment dummy, its canvas torso covered in writing, too smudged to read. Agata took off her coat and hung it on the dummy. She lit a cigarette, and started to eat one of the rolls. She threw the other one to me. It was rock hard. I nibbled at it, but was used to finer things: my parents were grocers and I took pleasure in eating. For Agata, eating seemed like a distracting chore. She ate the bread roll with such indifference it could have been a raw potato or a marrow bone, she wouldn't have noticed.

After she finished it, and her cigarette, she rubbed her large, bony hands together and tore the blanket off the object in the centre of the attic.

A gigantic black insect. It was a sewing machine, an old malicious one, black and gold, attached to its own desk with a treadle underneath, wrought metal like the grates over fire stoves and sewers. I was dumbfounded. Was she going to show me something both intricate and hideous that she had made? I knew from home economics class that she was a good sewer. If we finished a project before class was over, our teacher would make us mend her husband's socks, shirts, trousers and underwear. Agata was the only one who didn't mind doing it; she was so indifferent to whatever cloth she was feeding the machine, and it was against her nature to sew deliberately slowly like the rest of us. So she pumped out, with spiritless speed, flat doppelgängers of the teacher's husband, the yellow pads of her tobacco-stained finger -tips waltzing across the often unclean fabric which smelled like meat, soup, fruity liquors and that fried-onions-and-mushroom scent which oozes from the bodies of grown men, as if they were nothing but sacks of unwanted leftovers. Our home economics teacher was sour-looking and had a moustache. Some of us believed her husband was imaginary, that she'd bring the newly sewn pieces home, fill them with slops and potatoes so they'd gain life-like proportions, and lie in bed with her creation, kissing it until the seams ripped, then bringing the pieces, ripped and stained with exaggeration, back to school with domestic pride, as if her husband was too large, too important, too filthy, too manly for her alone to manage.

At the sight of Agata's sewing machine, my imagination whirred.

Agata would make me a pair of stockings I wouldn't be able to take off. A pair that would swallow my legs and expand three-dimensionally with their own horrible breath, like balloons, that followed the direction of her will. She would cut me and sew me back up again like the baby toads she dissected with cold expertise in science class.

'My mother's old sewing machine, but that's not all,' she said.

I looked closer.

There was a large mason jar where the spool was supposed to go, perched on top of the sewing machine like a translucent egg being expelled from its body. Inside the jar was a cylindrical light bulb, the sepia colour of old photographs. Emerging from the top was a brown wire, attached like a thread to the levers and regulators before vanishing into a short wooden box where the needle was supposed to be. The wire reappeared from a small hole on the side of the box, ending in a black earpiece, culled from a telephone. The box had faded writing on the side. CIGARS, it said.

Agata pushed over her armchair and sat in front of

the sewing machine. She started to pump the treadle. The large balance wheel started to turn, like a cinema reel. The jar started to move.

'Turn off the lights,' she said. I did, finding the switch near the door. The mason jar glowed. A wobbly bubble of light travelled across the room, then again, but this time there was some sort of shape inside it that was not fully formed, parts of it blacker than shadow, that morphed, flickering, into a Pierrot. He danced across the room. His face, white with black lips and eyebrows, was so beautiful I blushed. I blushed for him to see us, in Agata's filthy attic, our breath and armpits smelly from a day at school. His outfit was billowing white, with large black buttons, his feet small and pointed. I leaned against Agata's chair, watching the Pierrot circle us, again and again.

I knew what a Pierrot was. In my parents' shop, there was a porcelain Pierrot bust. He had rosy cheeks and the word PIERROT was written across his chest. His shoulders were covered in holes to put lollipops in. The lollipops did not sell very well; children were afraid of the strange, foreign man with his black skullcap. My father had brought the Pierrot at an antique shop and thought it lent an air of elegance to his business. We had no idea what the original lollipops were like, and imagined horrible and exotic flavours – crab, liquorice, goat, octopus – rising from the Pierrot's shoulders, the sugar spun into monstrous shapes.

Agata didn't know the word 'Pierrot'; I taught it to her, and she was visibly grateful. It suited the handsome, romantic figure in her attic much better than 'clown'.

Agata handed me the earpiece. I didn't hear anything. It was more like being listened to, as if there was a piece of shivering flesh behind the plastic. I didn't see the

Pierrot again, but this time appeared a man with white wings, wearing a striped sailor's shirt, and wide sailor's trousers. His hair was golden, greased back from his face, and his lips were red, very red, like he was wearing lipstick.

'I have never seen him before. I have only seen the Pierrot. This is why I wanted someone else to try it.' Agata put out her hand for the earpiece, pressed it to her ear, and the Pierrot appeared again. He performed a pirouette and blew us a kiss.

When she stopped treadling, I looked at the still jar. There were no images pasted onto it like on a lantern, or on the glass slides shown in class. I would have been disappointed if there had been: the winged man felt like something I had illustrated or brought into being.

Before Agata could start treadling again there was a knock on the door, a quiet, nervous tap. Without getting up from her chair, she gestured for me to open it and to turn on the light.

Her mother brought us cups of fake coffee made with chicory, and vanilla wafers that dissolved as soon as we put them in our mouths. Agata had a cigarette, then she told me to turn the light off again.

I didn't get home till late. My parents were pleased to hear I had been studying with Agata, for her intelligence was known around our whole village. The next morning I hoped, more than anything, that Agata would ask me to come over again. She did. I wasn't sure if she liked my company, or only wanted to see the 'angel' man again, but either way it didn't matter. I went every day, after school. Agata even borrowed a chair from her family's apartment for me to sit on. It was a toddler's chair, with short squat legs, the seat bedecked with colourful illustrations of dogs and flowers. Agata never let me pump the treadle of her machine.

By the time I went home each night I was starving, and my dinner, left on the table with a cloth on top, was lukewarm.

I was used to having a snack as soon as I got home from school, and I got into the habit of stealing things from my family's shop for Agata and me to eat. I brought hazelnut wafers, caramel chews, soft iced-ginger cookies, dry sausages, bottles of raspberry syrup we mixed with water, preserved plums covered in chocolate and, at Agata's request, an expensive brand of cigarettes with a picture of Romeo and Juliet on the packet, imported from a country in the Caribbean.

My father noticed I was taking things, and though he was glad I was studying (it was easy to lie to him about that), he couldn't afford such indulgences, and from then on only allowed me to take food from the overstock room. It was full of large jars of plum jam, dark brown in colour, and tinned sardines. Besides the cigarettes, it didn't make much difference to Agata. We ate the plum jam straight from the jar using spoons. I hated sardines, but Agata ate them, peeling off the silver skin and spitting out the bones.

·

My parents and I lived above our shop. We didn't share any walls with neighbours, and I was fascinated by Agata's building. It reminded me of the cabinet with dozens of tiny drawers where my parents kept precious seeds and spices. I became obsessed by the fantasy that the angel and Pierrot lived somewhere in the building, that their images had travelled through pipes and oozed through the attic walls like leaking water. When I

81

confessed it to Agata, she called me an idiot, but I couldn't concentrate on the machine until she'd introduced me to every neighbour. Every door was a disappointing drawer, full of tiny sticky flecks and withered cinnamon sticks. A breath of hope before the next one, then again, nothing. Finally, every room in the building had been emptied of my dreams, except the attic. I also begged her to let me see inside the cigar box. It was nothing to me; a tangle of wires and cogs, no tiny Pierrot and angel trapped inside like beautiful white mice in a cage.

The moving images came from us, or were connected to us, Agata couldn't say exactly. She had made the machine in order to project images from her mind's eye, but the Pierrot wasn't anything she had seen or imagined before. The angel was just as new to me.

I remembered once visiting my aunt in the city, when she took me to an arcade where a fortune teller lived in a theatrical box with glass sides. The fortune teller, who wore a colourful turban and many jewels, was made from wax, with a silent wax mouth. If you put a coin in a slot underneath the glass, she released a tiny card with your future written on it. Mine said I would get married and have one child. Agata's machine must have said something about our futures, for where else could the images come from?

I created beautiful and ridiculous scenarios in my mind. I was married to the angel, Agata to the Pierrot. The angel and I owned a small, white dog. I spent hours imagining how he would bathe without getting his wings wet, how I would stroke them and keep all the feathers that fell off in a red lacquered box.

I even dreamed that Agata's Pierrot was secretly in love with me, that he was in a sense enslaved by her. In fact, he felt somehow originally mine, because of the

82

Pierrot bust in my parents' shop. I knew the word, and had given it to her.

I knew Agata had fantasies too, but hers were perhaps filled with more knowledge of the world. Just as she knew how to smoke cigarettes without coughing and read foreign languages, so could she construct an imaginary marriage much more thorough than mine.

Sometimes she would suddenly say, 'Leave now.' The light continued moving after I left – I could see it under the door where I would stand until my legs hurt. I know she wanted to view the images in private. I never complained, I was too afraid of being banned from her machine forever. There was something in the way she said it – 'Leave' – that made her seem more grown up than me. Yet we were dependent on each other like a pair of twins, conjoined by a dream rather than a body, for the angel appeared more often when I held the machine to my ear, and the Pierrot when she did. The machine, our secret, bound us together: I could tell her parents or our classmates, while she could tell my parents I wasn't studying.

We weren't friends, exactly. I was bothered by the sound of her breathing and sniffing, she always had a runny nose, and she often screamed at me for sucking my teeth or for noisily passing gas. Our bodies were nuisances to the enjoyment of the machine. I asked my father if I could borrow his record player, which folded up neatly into a suitcase. Music greatly enhanced the whole experience as it made it seem like our dear friends were not silent and unbreathing but, like us, merely drowned out by the music.

The colour of the attic's walls, the greyish pink wallpaper with its pattern of green ferns curled like little goblins' ears, gave the angel and Pierrot the appearance of having a skin disease. I didn't notice this detail in my initial enchantment, but it became noticeable as I demanded more from the machine, like a stomach expanding from eating an ever-increasing amount of food.

I had the idea of painting the walls white, but Agata didn't approve – it would mean days away from the machine, she didn't want paint to get on her books, she didn't want to pack up her things – so I constructed a white collage along her walls using a white linen tablecloth, a large white blouse of my mother's, some sheets of typing paper, cloth bags for sugar and flour from the grocery store, endpapers ripped out of books, a piece of wooden board I painted white myself and carried over. Any white scrap I could find. Agata agreed: the angel and Pierrot looked purer, fuller, against white.

I had a dream that I removed all my teeth and glued them to the walls. I removed Agata's teeth too, but they were stained and crooked, as in real life. As soon as I extracted them they started to grow until they were the size and length of elephant tusks. They smelled like soiled laundry and were covered in tiny black cavities.

Once, Large Barbara tried to follow us home, as if she could smell we were up to something important. We ran, Large Barbara's cane rattling against the stones of the streets behind us. It was a horrible cane, with a doll's head on the top, soiled and squished by Large Barbara's sweaty hand. She screamed and screamed, irregular sounds, like the varied contents of a small, travelling menagerie, her cane a large beak or claw hitting the bars. She couldn't catch up.

We didn't mention the incident once we were upstairs, but the attic contained a thought too repellent to voice: what would Large Barbara, who was hopeless, an idiot, see with her ear against the machine? If she were to see, for example, a beautiful prince, wearing turquoise trousers and a yellow sash, it would mean the machine had no base in the future, or reality, and was nothing more than a reflection of our desires.

.

I don't remember the date of the day Mr Magnolia first appeared. All days had melted into each other, into an amber-coloured syrup that slowly hardened under the whirring of Agata's machine.

I do remember that Agata was holding the earpiece the first time Mr Magnolia appeared.

He was bald, except for a thin rim of hair like scum on a dirty bowl and a plain, unfanciful moustache shaped like the little plastic combs used for lice searches at school. He was old, like a father, and wore a suit, a drab, ill-fitting grey one.

As he moved across the room he sneered, stuck his tongue out and grabbed his crotch, his mouth open in a silent laugh.

We both gasped, but Agata didn't stop treadling her machine.

The next round, the Pierrot reappeared, as if nothing had changed; then my angel, then Pierrot and the strange old man again, in an odd, nonsensical sequence.

Agata kept pumping, horrified and transfixed.

'Mr Magnolia,' she whispered, then added, 'The name came to me as he appeared. They must come from the same place, they must belong to each other.'

'I don't know, I heard that word somewhere, yes, it's his name.'

She looked the word up in her seven-volume dictionary. The different volumes were scattered around her attic and it took us a while to find L-M. We were surprised to learn that MAGNOLIA was a flower, a large pink or white one. The dictionary did not contain pictures or any more information, so we could only imagine how horrible the flower must be. We went to a flower shop.

'Do you have any magnolias?' I stumbled over the word, unsure if we were being obscene.

'Magnolia grows on trees, I can't sell a bushel of them. I have beautiful purple asters, poppies, carnations, roses. Silly girls, magnolias grow on trees!' said the shop owner, a broad woman with dyed hair and too much make-up, wearing a wet and stained apron over her dress.

Agata blushed at the word 'silly'. It was the first time I had ever seen her blush.

'Here, I'll show you a picture.' The shop owner went into the back of her shop, returning with a large, damp book.

'It can either be white, or pink. Girls, it grows on trees in foreign places!' she laughed. The flower looked like a dessert.

'Stupid, worthless dictionary. It should've told us that,' Agata mumbled as we left. We walked back to her house in a hurry, both wanting to see Mr Magnolia again, to compare him with the image of the flower we had just seen. But there was no resemblance between the beautiful, large flower and the ugly plainness of Mr Magnolia, who grimaced at us and tugged at his trouser legs.

'Mr Magnolia, he must come from abroad. That is the connection. Perhaps he has an important message,' said Agata when we were back in her attic.

We recorded and tried to decode all his poses, gestures and faces, but it was really a way to kill time between seeing the Pierrot or the angel who struck us dumb. Whatever music was playing when Mr Magnolia appeared was made ridiculous. We could never play that song again. As Mr Magnolia continued to appear, more and more songs were ruined. I borrowed more records from my father's collection – symphonies, ballets, operas, folk songs – and was careless with the ones we no longer wanted, tossing them across the attic. They cracked and were forgotten.

Sometimes Agata would say, 'I am so sick of Mr Magnolia, thank you very much,' or 'Fuck you and your Mr Magnolia,' her lips curled, her head turned in my direction.

It was unfair of her to blame me for Mr Magnolia. He first appeared when the earpiece was held against her head. He slithered out of her mind like a maggot. Was he waiting to prance, like a devil, into both of our futures?

I lost weight, I smelled like tobacco. I was behind on my schoolwork. My teachers had written my parents a letter, so they knew. Agata wasn't. She didn't hand in assignments anymore either, but I think the teachers believed she could do no wrong; they were firm in the belief that her work would be the best in class if she handed it in, so it wasn't necessary for her to do so. She didn't speak in class anymore, but sat sullenly, her arms crossed, one foot underneath her desk moving up and down as if pressing an invisible treadle.

Neither of us had appetites, our stomachs felt tight and curled like unblossomed flowers. We consumed only cigarettes, cups of black tea and spoonfuls of plum jam, brown and glistening like grease to smooth the cogs of a machine.

One evening, returning home bleary-eyed, my

fingers sticky, my parents forbade me from returning to Agata's. My mother said it was disgusting for a family to have so many children, and that she had heard they all slept in one big bed, boys and girls mixed. My mother picked me up from school the next day, and the next, and also dropped me off in the morning. The first night away from Agata's machine, I couldn't sleep.

'What happened?' I asked Agata as soon as we were seated in class.

'Nothing. The same. Mr Magnolia appeared fifty times, Pierrot twenty times.'

'And my angel?'

'Not once. He only appears when you are in the room.'

The thought gave me relief and hope. Had the angel missed me? Did he not think it worth appearing if I wasn't there?

Still, I worried he would appear for Agata alone the next day. Every morning I asked her, and she gave the same reply. After four days, she answered, 'Yes. He blew me a kiss.'

'No. I'm joking,' she snorted, when my face gave away my horror.

After a week, I stopped asking her, though she still told me. I acted indifferent, and it started to make me feel indifferent.

I felt calmer, more focused. I could read, do my homework. My appetite returned, my parents indulging whatever edible whims I had.

The time came, a few weeks later, when I felt assured that I could see Agata's machine again without the intensity of feeling I had before.

I was even glad at the thought of seeing Mr Magnolia, but mostly I was curious to see how my reappearance would affect the expressions of the angel and Pierrot.

Of course, my parents wouldn't let me, so I had to sneak out after dark. I was sure Agata would be running her machine throughout the night, and I was right. The angel and Pierrot didn't act any differently than before; I was disappointed, I had expected them to jump off the wall and embrace me. All I could do was continue holding the earpiece to my scalp, for Agata to continue pumping. There was a jar of plum jam left over from my last visit, viscid because the cap hadn't been put back on properly. We ate it from the jar with our fingers, the earpiece increasingly sticky as we passed it between us.

'Faster! Move it faster!' I screamed, Mr Magnolia disappearing as quickly as he appeared, his image not fully formed, his head oddly squished and wobbly.

I barely focused on my angel when he appeared, so keen to see him a second time. 'C'mon, again!' I screamed as he was pulled back into the lantern. I kicked away my little chair, sat on Agata's lap and put my foot over hers, adding pressure. My foot was much smaller, it didn't make her go any faster, but she put her free arm around my waist and held me there, and the earpiece passed seamlessly between us. The angel and Pierrot became stronger, more flamboyant in their actions. The angel imitated the obscene crotch-grabbing of Mr Magnolia, and I was so thrilled that at first I did not hear my father shouting in the hall. I did not hear him until he had grabbed me, and was carrying me away, and only then I noticed that my legs and arms and nightdress were covered in jam, so dark it could have been blood. Perhaps my father imagined it was.

At home, my mother bathed me, calling me disgusting over and over again, while I moaned, a strange, deep sound I had never made before. I did not go to school the next day; I did not go to that school ever again. I suffered from horrible visions: Agata's lips, Mr Magnolia's crotch, jars of jam with bits and pieces of sewing machines hidden inside that I choked on, they tasted like metal and liquorice. I kicked and screamed and threw up, and was kept in my room for months.

·

When I could get out of bed, I was sent to stay with my aunt in the city. My parents sold the shop and joined me a few months later. By then I was so integrated into my aunt's exciting city life that our village, and my entire childhood, was a blur I was embarrassed to remember.

My aunt took me to restaurants, bookshops, department stores, markets and the cinema. She was a professor, and though she lived alone, she had many male friends. I became fond of one, Leopold. He was much older than me. He had a raspberry-coloured birthmark on his cheek and wore very tiny, round spectacles. I kept in touch with him throughout my schooling, and married him when I started university. Our son inherited his father's gigantic nose, which depressed Leopold sometimes, as his nose was full of cruel, bitter memories like an old heart, but I liked it. They both made me think of crows with their feathers painted pink.

I found work as an archivist and often looked for Agata's name in catalogues and newspapers, but I found no trace of her. I assumed she'd gone abroad, perhaps taken on a different name to fit in better. It was hard to return to our country, and I felt bad for her parents, who had put so much effort into supporting her, most likely getting nothing in return.

I still suffered, a little. I couldn't stand any sort of apparatus. Leopold once gave me a music box shaped like a theatre with a dancing paper Pierrot inside. It made me so nervous I had to run to the bathroom and vomit. I couldn't even hang a mobile above our son's crib because of the shadows it would project across his nursery walls.

I hated the microfilm readers at work, I avoided them as much as possible, and typewriters, which I used sparingly, always biting my tongue. I preferred to make handwritten labels and lists, and made sure my handwriting was neat and clear so my co-workers wouldn't complain. My favourite things to work with were old manuscripts, so old I had to wear white gloves while handling them, manuscripts written on skin.

I couldn't think about the way clothes were made, with those awful, black contraptions. I was drawn to expensive things described as 'hand woven', 'hand knitted'; I loved the word 'hand', its warm and soft connotations. I always imagined a chubby, pink child's hand like my son's, completely opaque – no wiry veins showing underneath.

I hated anything that whirled, flickered, buzzed, clicked, clattered. Sometimes I had nightmares, beasts with scissor mouths, metal fan wings, a telephone receiver for eyes, metal pincers and cog wheels longing to touch me.

There aren't any flattering photos of me. Cameras make me blink and shudder.

I still took great pleasure in food, with the exception of fish and jam. Fish did not seem natural, but mechanical somehow, perhaps because of their silver skins. I often had a dream in which Agata scooped out my flesh with a long spoon and stuffed it into fish skins made from silver satin and sewed the seams onto her machine. I was left as nothing but a pile of fake sardines, the satin damp from my flesh hidden inside, and a skeleton wearing my own hair as a wig.

For my birthday, Leopold always gave me cured ham legs, pickled tongues and other gourmet meats, ones that resembled what they were, meat that hadn't been minced, ground, pulverised.

When I was in my forties, I went back to our old village to visit a sick aunt who was too weak to travel to the city. I had the idea that I would also visit Agata's mother, remembering the cruel way I used to laugh at her bald patches, her skinny limbs. I also suspected my parents had given her harsh words. I wanted to show her that she was forgiven, that really it wasn't her fault. I would bring her flowers.

I looked for the old flower shop, but it was gone. There was a floral section in a large, new grocery store. I bought her a cheery orange bouquet.

The curtains in the first floor windows of their building were faded from the sun, and full of equally faded trinkets, like deteriorating daguerreotypes that took the interior life of the building with them as they crinkled and vanished, leaving nothing but a blank stone wall, an uninhabited ruin.

I was surprised to find anyone there. Agata's mother answered their door.

She wore a turban made of ragged grey and black fabric, from which I surmised that she must be entirely bald underneath. She was even thinner than I remembered, and bent, like a rib bone. The apartment was free of children; they were all grown up by now. Instead there was an old man, huddled in a chair by the stove, giving off the same sopping smell as a toddler. I wondered how many of their children had left the town, how many had left our country, to which they could never return.

'Come upstairs,' her mother said in a whisper, placing the flowers on the table. Agata's father flared his nostrils, seeking the origin of the floral smell, and I realized that he was blind.

'From the glass. His eyes were ruined by the glass,' Agata's mother said, shuffling out. I followed her up the stairs. There was a distinctive mixture of aromas – cabbages, shoe polish, mice, tobacco, old kitchen pipes, walnuts, smoked ham – as if the stairwell was an accordion, and each step a key that released not a note, but a heavy spray of fragrance. It was the thought of being trapped in that wheezing, terrible contraption that made me hesitate, but Agata's poor mother kept walking up, and so I followed. Strongest was a warm, waxy smell. It drowned out all the others in great, deep waves, and I had the sensation I was ascending towards a room full of thousands of burning tallow candles.

By the time I glimpsed the buttery light under the door, I knew what to expect, and my ears took in the flickering sound.

She sat in the same armchair. She was so fat that her eyes, which used to protrude, were sunk deep into the flesh of her face, as if they were drowning in the bluish purple bags below them. She was lumpy and frayed, like a cloth doll stuffed with too much wool. Unclean fleece, I thought, torn from an animal. Her brown hair was cut short, and was oily. I could see layers of dandruff flakes stuck to her hairline, glistening in the light of her lantern, like shards of broken glass among the wooden ruins of a building. In the centre was a bald spot; an unclean skylight, cracked like a boiled egg tapped with a spoon, but still solid.

'The angel hasn't come back since you left. He is waiting for you,' she said, only half-looking at me and her mother, who whispered, 'I'll bring you girls some coffee in a few hours,' and left.

My white collage on the wall had turned yellow. Scraps of fresh paper, mostly toilet roll, ribbons and a fridge door had been added. It resembled a frilled and bedraggled wedding dress, ill-preserved by its bride, worn over and over again, the sweat and sweetness of the wedding day covered in grey reproductions of itself, the stains of a day relived over and over. I imagined the attic as one of the arched hollows under the bride's arm, the place where the body leaves its imprint on fabric most intensely, those pathetic, damp and silent mouths of the heart.

My old chair was very small, it hurt my back, the ear-piece was greasy, but I felt behind it that strange piece of flesh, that mysterious ear listening to me. Once more my winged man appeared, wearing the same appealing wide-wool trousers, the same lipstick, and I thought, he's feigning cheery indifference, he is yellowed and worn by my absence.

RHINOCEROS

Across from the apartment building where Nicholas and I lived was a train station. There weren't any trains, but a café whose small metal chairs were spread out across the vast space, and a kiosk. The kiosk sold navy blue gloves, packages of powder you put in water to make colourful sweet drinks, syrup that did the same thing, pads of grey paper and sea monkey kits, nylon stockings that smelled like chemicals and broke into holes as soon as you put them on, small jars of salt, and bars of pink candy that were very waxy in consistency and came in a package with a goofy, yellow animal with long ears represented on it. Everyone knew what a rabbit was, even if they had never seen one, because of that candy. I thought, if Nicholas were an animal he'd be a rabbit like that. He was small, and almost albino.

Nicholas and I went to the station often, because it had speakers which played music, very faintly, and there were old, interesting posters on the walls: a large poster for the film *Peculiar Jane*, one for a dark imported beer – the beer bottle was surrounded by crows – and another poster of a winged insect made out of metal or something. That one was for a jewellery shop that was no longer open. We had written down the address and visited, but there was no sign of it ever being a jewellery shop: in its place was a closed-down bakery filled with empty bread shelves. Nicholas had sketched and painted the posters many times. The station was very draughty, lukewarm teas from the café didn't help much, but we were used to being cold. The very old brick fireplace in our living room had been filled in with an electric one that didn't work. It had strange white bars covered in fuzzy-looking red wires behind a metal bar grate. It looked

97

like a very bad drawing of a real fire. The hearth was covered in beautiful tiles with green flowers on them. Once, when desperate, we tore one of the tiles off and sold it. It didn't get us more than two cups of tea however, and we became so nervous about the landlord discovering the missing tile that Nicholas painted a replica on hard paper and glued it in the empty space. One could hardly tell the difference, as long as they didn't step on it.

Above, on the mantelpiece, Nicholas kept his sea monkeys in a plastic, castle-shaped aquarium. They were tiny grey things, they resembled aquatic bed bugs, really. The water was murky. I had bought them for Nicholas's birthday. The package had pink creatures with chimpanzee-like faces and clear roles – mother, father, son, daughter, wearing fancy outfits. In his childish way, Nicholas was disappointed that the creatures didn't resemble the image at all but he still painted them, using a magnifying glass.

Beside the aquarium was a mantel clock that looked like a shrunken train station, a small, long skull – the person we bought it from said it was a rat's – and two winking-face tea cups Nicholas had inherited from his grandmother. We didn't use them because Nicholas thought they would scream if we poured hot liquid into their heads.

Directly across from the fireplace was a red couch with some sort of botanical design on it. It was inside the couch that I found the beef can, after removing the cushions and cleaning underneath because the couch sometimes gave off an odd smell. The can had a white animal on it, called a beef. Nicholas became terribly excited. He opened the can with a knife, thinking there would be a tiny beef inside that looked like the one on the cover. It was just horrid, blackish mush inside – it smelled wicked. I said, Nicholas we ought to throw it out, it might be dangerous, and he threw the stuff out but kept the lid, washed it off, and painted it many times. I had encountered the word 'beef' in novels before. It was something English people often ate, but I didn't know what it looked like till now, and the novels were now half ruined by the image of the characters eating that black, smelly substance.

Every five months, a man in a grey top hat visited to pick up Nicholas's paintings and drawings. He loved the one of the beef, saying it was very noble, and asked where we had found the image. Nicholas showed him the tin lid.

We found it on the street, Nicholas said. The man replied he'd like to have it too if we didn't mind, and put the lid in his pocket, saying, I haven't seen one of those since I was a boy. We weren't sure if he meant the animal or the tin.

Don't worry, Nicholas said, after the man left, I kept a sketch of the beef just for us, it's in the suitcase under the bed.

That suitcase also contained some drawings of me, kept hidden because we were under obligation to give all of Nicholas's artworks to the man in the top hat, though I don't think the man would've liked them. He never acknowledged or expressed interest in me, only in Nicholas and his paintings of sea monkeys, pots, insects and whatever else he could find.

He gave us money, and sometimes food, in exchange for the artworks. The food was never consistent, for example, he brought us two bags full of greenish-brown grapes. We ate as much as we could. Some of them were mouldy and shrivelled, which gave Nicholas the idea we could make raisins out of them. The air of the apartment turned out to be too damp for them to turn into raisins, though we did hold them over the stove for some time.

Another time, he brought us a large sack of flour. I didn't know what to do with it, I made a dreadful white soup out of it that gave us both stomach aches, but fortunately we were able to sell the rest of the sack at a market we went to every week to look for treasures. Nicholas was always looking for bits of animal, but someone sold him a jagged piece of broken porcelain saying it was a bone, he didn't have a good eye for such things. I found the rat's skull, and traded a nice blue dress I had for it. My only other clothes were a brown skirt with white spots on it, a black skirt with pink and green flowers, and some shirts and jumpers Nicholas and I shared, mainly inherited from his grandmother. Whenever the man in the grey top hat visited, Nicholas made me put on a pink jumper – the only one without paint stains on it, though it did have a large moth hole on the chest covered with a badge that used to say 'VOTE MAXIMILLIAN' on it. We thought this phrase might be dangerous so we blacked it out with paint. It just looked like a large black button.

We showed Nicholas's paintings in the living room, the light there was good. We also had a studio room for Nicholas, a bedroom, a bathroom with a large green tub, and a dining room we didn't use as we didn't have a table, and there was a foreboding-looking light fixture dangling from the ceiling.

Sometimes the market had picture books wrapped in plastic, but we couldn't afford them so we tried to memorize the images on the cover, a hairy animal wearing a straw hat, a pink one in overalls, a large grey house. Nicholas quickly drew them all after we left, but the results were frightening, too frightening to paint, we thought. The animals just looked like misshapen people.

It took us almost two hours to walk to the art supplies store. We walked arm in arm.

One old man lived above us, the only other person in the whole building, he owned a bicycle. I tried to be friendly to him, bringing him some tubers and tea, but he never offered to lend us the bicycle though Nicholas and I always looked so tired when we returned home. The old man didn't use the bicycle often, only once a week or so to buy bread or a bottle of spirits, which he put under his arms while cycling but never dropped.

I pictured Nicholas and me on the bicycle often, me pedalling, him sitting on the back with his arms around my waist.

I always packed us a lunch for our trip to the art store: a thermos of tea and some boiled tubers wrapped in foil. We stopped somewhere nice, a statue, a fountain with no water in it, to eat. We also had to stop for Nicholas to cough more often than I liked, but Nicholas wouldn't let me go alone. He insisted we go together though it exhausted him. I think he was also afraid of me choosing the wrong things.

Whenever we went out Nicholas brought his net, just in case he saw an insect or something. There were three cockroaches taped to the wall of his studio room which he had found in the halls of our building, and a bed bug kept in a velvet box. When we ate at home he was deliberately messy, hoping to attract something living.

On one of our walks to the art supply shop we discovered a cavernous grocery store. We could hear our feet echoing as we walked through it. Not all the lights were turned on, so we just went into the aisles that were lit up.

There were shelves and shelves of tea, all the boxes were quite faded and old-looking, and the tins rusty. That was about all, I think the shop also had some cotton kitchen cloths, dusty bottles of syrup and some dried white things – we didn't know what they were.

Does tea go off? I asked Nicholas. He said he didn't think so, so we bought a few of the cheapest boxes, I was afraid of the rust on the tins. As we felt so abundant in tea, Nicholas used some of it to do paintings of his cockroaches on paper. They looked like light brown watercolour pictures, very lovely, but the next time we went by the grocery store it was closed, shuttered up.

The art supply shop was squished between two vegetable shops. There were mildewy curtains drawn across the windows that had become stuck to and stained by a handful of dead, brown plants, giving the unpleasant impression of a healing wound and bandages. It was half empty. There were small plaster busts of men with beards and lots of boxes of chalk.

Sometimes it took the owner a long time to find the paints Nicholas wanted. Nicholas always became nervous that there wouldn't be any more, that he'd have to start drawing with chalk, which gave him a funny, unpleasant feeling to touch, and which you could just wipe away.

The store had lots of nice paper. Sometimes Nicholas tried to buy me some, but I said no, the grey paper pads from the train station kiosk were fine enough for me.

The last time we were there, the owner had hardly any paint left and wasn't sure if he could get more, but told us there was another art supply store if you walked along the train tracks until you were at a station with a green roof, walked through it, or around it if the doors were locked, and then on a few streets from there. He drew us a map, but couldn't say how long it would take, though it was sure to have more supplies as it was so out-of-the-way. Nicholas was enthusiastic about making the journey, but I was worried about his health. It could take hours, or days even, and what if they had nothing but white chalk?

I dug up a bunch of tubers and made them into pancakes for our trip. There was a small lot behind the building, I grew tubers there, when we first moved in it had been overgrown with sinister ferns. I put the pancakes, a bar of rabbit candy and some jumpers in a bag. I made Nicholas wear the scarf.

We never made it to the other art supplies store because we discovered a zoo on the way. We stopped in one of the stations along the tracks to eat lunch, there was even a tea machine which served tea in tiny plastic cups. On one of the walls was a map of the neighbourhood, and it said 'ZOO HERE' with an arrow. There was no one tending the zoo, the ticket booth was empty, so we just walked in. Nicholas was shaking.

All the cages were empty, of course. Leaves, puddles and eroded concrete, but each cage had a sign with an illustration of the animal that had once lived there, and information on what they had liked to eat and where they were from. That's the rhinoceros then, he said, the elephant, the zebra. He made sketches from the illustrations. As I couldn't draw, I wrote *Zebra* in my notebook three times for emphasis, as that was the animal I liked most.

Nicholas was too tired and excited from the zoo for us to continue on our way to the art supply store.

We went back to the zoo the next day, Nicholas couldn't rest until we did. He frantically sketched all sorts of beasts and winged creatures. All the illustrations were in black and white, we didn't know what colours to paint them, Nicholas decided to paint them pink and brown like humans. The rhinoceros horn obsessed him.

Was it like the rat's skull, or a fingernail?

He decided to grow one of his fingernails long to know how to paint it, thinking a rhinoceros horn was probably like some sort of thick fingernail. It looked grotesque, and he let it get very dirty. I was relieved when he cut it off. He wanted to add it to his collection on the mantelpiece, but I convinced him that it might disgust or offend the man in the grey top hat, so he put it on the bathroom windowsill.

I was looking at it from the bathtub, I think it had started to curl from the condensation, when something came out of me, a pink lump. It was flat on the ends, like a tuber with the tips sliced off. It had no mouth, eyes, or hands, but it was alive: it was struggling in the water. I grabbed it and put it on my stomach. When I stood up, it squirmed so much I almost dropped it. It was soft, boneless. I wrapped it in a towel, like I had seen babies wrapped, and held it. There wasn't any blood.

Nicholas was painting. I crouched in the dining room holding the thing. I fell asleep, and when I woke up it was still, and strangely hardened. I hadn't figured out how to feed it or anything. Perhaps I couldn't.

The lamp I didn't like was swinging to and fro.

I didn't want Nicholas to paint the thing, or even to see it. I wrapped it in a green scarf I didn't like to wear and put it in a porcelain jar that said 'Mustard' on it and had always been empty. Nicholas was asleep comfortably in bed, a smear of white paint on his face.

I felt agitated, however, with it sitting in the pantry with all our food. I didn't want to bury it in the yard in case I later mistook it for a tuber. The next time we were getting ready to go to the zoo, I stuffed it in a small beaded purse I had, it was all withered and darkened. At the zoo, I wandered off as Nicholas was sketching a wolf.

I unwrapped the thing, and threw it between the bars of the zebra cage. It landed just on the peripheries of a puddle. I wished it were more hidden, but perhaps it would roll away, or leaves would cover it eventually.

When I returned to Nicholas, he had stopped drawing, and was crouched over, coughing. What if Nicholas expired and dried up like the thing that had come out of me? Then what would I do? I helped him up and we returned home, though he hadn't finished his drawing. He had only done the wolf's head, floating in the space of the paper like an abandoned hat.

THE SAD TALE OF THE SCONCE

The ship swayed back and forth on the sea like a cross between a cradle and a rowdy tavern. The wooden mermaid on its tip was a welcoming sign: gin and hard work for those with feet, death to those with tails.

Among the ship's catch that afternoon were a magnificent orange octopus, silver and green fish, black eels, seaweed, glass bottles, small turtles, and chunks of red coral and jellyfish. The catch was a multitude of colours and textures, like the thigh of an old debauched prince squished into a stocking, the bulbous head of the octopus a blister ripe with pus.

How delicious it would be roasted, the sailors cried, but the captain stopped them: a zoo in Berlin or Moscow would buy the octopus and they would all be rich. In the zoo, it would wear a bowtie and make love to women pretending to be mermaids, the captain told his crew, redirecting their appetites. They made eel stew for dinner, and put the octopus in a bucket filled with water, with a lid on top.

The fishes disappeared during the night as the sailors, one by one, stole them away to their bunk beds, intoxicated enough that the small, wet creatures were adequate substitutes for women. By morning, scales covered their sheets, and the octopus was gone. After removing itself from the bucket and sliding across the deck, it quickly copulated with the mermaid figurehead on the tip of the ship before diving back into the sea.

The seeds of the octopus were very slowly saturated into the wooden mermaid.

She spent many more years at sea before the ship was taken apart, the wood of its belly turned into houses and bonfires, and the more precious parts, including the mermaid, donated to a museum where she was confined to the darkness of the storage rooms.

The sconce grew out of his mother very slowly, the way a tree grows roots, branches and gnarls, and dropped from her tail like a chestnut onto the shelf. As objects are all born with purposes, this one was born to be a sconce. The sconce had a cherub face surrounded by writhing wooden limbs which ended in two little bowls, too small for eggs, but the perfect fit for candles, which the sconce longed for with mysterious anticipation, to rid himself of the feeling of being empty-handed.

They lived in cool darkness, and sometimes light. His mother, in her silent wooden way, told him about the sea, and fishes, and sailors, and the octopus with orange arms who was his father. Once, they were taken out of the storage rooms for an exhibition on marine culture. The museum staff could find no trace of the sconce in the catalogues, and saw it as an administrative misstep. He was some bit of old ship, a decorative pustule. His mother was very much admired, her paint retouched before she went on view. Everything was so splendid, the sconce almost imagined himself as having been part of the same boat as his mother, an interior adornment illuminating the ship's intestines.

Many viewers remarked that they could almost smell the sea, the exhibition was so vivid. The smell became stronger as the sconce aged: it was his inheritance from his father. Museum staff scoured the room looking for dead insects and rodents, and secretly accused each other of using the room for romantic meetings and oily snacks of olives and sardines. For a while there was no one. The lights were never turned on. The sconce nibbled on his memories of the exhibition, and his mother told him again and again in her silent wooden way about ships, octopuses and oceans. They had almost forgotten about the rest of the museum above and around them when an emaciated member of staff unlocked the door, sniffed, his nostrils flaring, and grabbed the little sconce. The man licked the sconce's arms, and rubbed a piece of hard black bread across the sconce's face, as if it were butter and not wood, before stuffing the bread into his mouth. He was about to put the sconce into a pigskin briefcase he brought with him and —

Boom boom boom!

The top of the museum was blown away, destroyed like a cake eaten by hungry children. Dusty light and scraps of oil paintings poured into the storage room and the staff member was buried underneath an iron anchor. A trail of soldiers dressed in grey marched in, looking for food (someone thought they had smelled salt and fish), jewels, anything. One soldier kissed the mermaid, leaving a rancid spot of spittle glistening on her lips. He had a child at home and the little face of the sconce made him sentimental, so he put it and the mermaid into his rucksack, a little make-believe wife and child to fondle until the war ended. All the soldiers in their makeshift camp admired her – they were starved for women – and a woman made of wood with a fish's tail would do.

The soldiers came from a land of equality and sharing, and so the mermaid was passed around. Her wooden breasts were sucked and whittled down by the crude teeth and tongues of various soldiers, until there was nothing left but splinters and flakes of pink paint. They ate her lips, her hair, her shoulders, and, using a knife, gave her the anatomy a mermaid does not have, two rather small green legs, that were meant to be a woman's but resembled a frog's. They stuck wet rags between them, and it did fine for some.

There was one soldier who became fixated on the sconce, still in fine condition compared to his mother. 'A nice sweet face, those cheeks, and tiny lips,' he said, removing it from the other soldier's rucksack one night, and emptying his desires onto the sconce's face. He wiped the sconce off with a red hanky, and placed him back among the other soldier's things. He continued to secretly borrow the sconce until the war was over.

The sconce was brought home from the war and for the first time, he became an actual sconce. The soldier nailed him to the wall, and his wife stuck two dripping candles on his writhing wooden limbs. The candles were more painful than the sconce had imagined them to be, and left black marks on his cheeks.

There was a child in the house, the child for whom the sconce was a substitute during the war. He was a little cruel thing and would take the candles out of their cups and hold the flame directly against the sconce's eyes.

The child complained that the sconce gave him nightmares. In truth, he was jealous, and did not want another child's face in the house, even a wooden one. His temper grew as his mother's stomach rose, and the former soldier took the sconce away so that he could have a good night's sleep.

He brought the sconce to a small stone house with a high ceiling and a tower. The house belonged to a fat man with a grey beard who wore black dresses. The walls of the house were covered in faces like his own, wooden faces, but also faces of gold, silver, stone and wax. There were candles everywhere, plants and strange ornate metal bottles that released nice smelling smoke. The sconce's scent became unnoticeable among the many smells of the stone house, wax, smoke and rosemary (which the sconce did not know by name but came to love).

People came in, now and then, to sing unevenly, to kiss each other and to eat little meals – a sip of something, a small piece of bread, an onion. Often, the soldier's family came, and seemed to be larger each time.

One day the large man in a black dress died and another large man in a black dress came to live in the same house. The new man had a blond beard instead of a grey one, and when no one was visiting, slept on the wooden guest chairs and drank by himself. Once, he ate a crinkled burnt fish while he drank, and left the bones on the floor.

The sconce told the fish bones how his father had come from the sea, and he had heard about fishes, but the fish bones didn't say anything in return and were carried away by mice. Some of the stone and wooden faces were carried away too, not by mice but by the large man. They didn't return. The man grew larger and redder and the sconce wondered if he ate them the way he had eaten that fish.

The time came for the sconce to be taken away. He was put in a sack and taken to a shop filled with old things. The bearded man left with a little bag of coins and the sconce was put on a shelf with a clown, a tin dog and a vase.

The shop was teeming with unclean life: moths, spiders, rats, worms, fleas, who gobbled each other and things in the shop which were covered in tasty layers of use: a crumb here, a tea leaf in the bottom of an old kettle, a mutton juice stain on a doll's dress which still tasted of something when chewed, a chocolate forgotten in a black lacquered box.

The clown was made of cloth and the sconce saw him nibbled on by rats until there was almost nothing left, save for his porcelain hands which the sconce dreamed of placing in his candle-holes to use as his own.

The sconce himself was visited by wood-worms, who tunnelled deep inside him. He could not move his mouth or his cheeks but in his soul giggled at the sensation. Their consumption of him felt tender.

The owner of the shop was covered in fleas. He looked like a very small lamb, with glasses. He reminded the sconce of a painting from the museum, with two little babies and a lamb in it, surrounded by stars. One evening, the little lamb man put on a beret and a little red rucksack and left forever. The store had been sold to a new owner, a little fat man who smelled like perfume and liked to eat tinned oysters with a special little golden fork.

He cleaned the store with a feather duster and mop. He polished all the surfaces. He put traps everywhere for the rodents, and poison for the worms and fleas. After the worms disappeared, the sconce could feel air pass through the hollows where they had lived, and he felt lonely. The store was brightly lit and smelled like lavender and oysters. The fat little man cleaned the sconce with orange oil to hide his scent, which the fat little man rather guiltily blamed on his own oyster breath.

During a busy holiday season, a man wearing a white suit with a fresh red soup stain on it and a woman wearing a hat covered in glass strawberries came in and bought the sconce along with an enamelled copper teapot and an amber brooch with an ugly bug trapped inside. The sconce was put in a trunk with postcards of fancy buildings and seashores, a paper parasol, the teapot and brooch, and taken first on a train, then a boat, the first boat he had ever been on – but of course he didn't know that because he was locked in the dark.

When they arrived at their destination he was hung on a wall covered in striped pink and gold paper in a dark and narrow house he couldn't picture from the outside. He was given fresh candles every few days and became very well acquainted with a clock across from him who only knew one word, and a painting of a young woman wearing a yellow dress.

The husband, who no longer wore white suits, but grey ones, often paused in the hall in front of the sconce, flaring his nose and twitching his moustache: 'The maid, I shall have to talk to the maid, eating sardines and not cleaning her hands again. I can smell traces of sardines on every surface she touches. Her fingers might as well be sardines.'[1]

When his wife passed by, she touched the seat of her skirt and then pressed her fingers to her nose, saying something odd, such as, 'It isn't that time of the month yet,' or, 'I thought it had passed.' She would then look fondly at the sconce, which had the face of a little boy.

He stayed with the husband and wife for many years,

[1] This actually once happened in the city of —, in the year 19—. A boy ate so many tinned sardines, greedily with his hands instead of a fork, that one morning he woke up to discover his fingers had turned into sardines desperately gasping for water. He could feel their tiny hearts throbbing like wounds. He plunged both hands into his nightstand jug of water. He had to keep his sardine-fingers in a bucket of water to keep them alive. A doctor designed two glass mittens for the child but failed to take into account the need not just for water, but for oxygen, and the fish died. Their corpses were removed before they rotted, leaving the boy with fingerless hands. For the rest of his life he kept the fish bones of his fingers in an old cigar box in the bottom of his wardrobe with a note requesting the fish bones be buried with him when he died. As an old man, he would often go into grocery stores, look at sardine in their fancy tins and quietly weep, like a mourner visiting the grave of their beloved.

and outstayed many maids who were accused of eating too many sardines. When the couple died the sconce was left to one of the maids, who loved it loyally and polished it with caster oil every week until she died. Her own child, a grown man with spider veins covering his nose, sold the sconce to an antique store, as the little face frightened him. He threw the money from the sale into a river. The sconce was displayed on a wall covered in paintings of ladies, oranges and chickens. There were many dolls in the shop with chubby faces like his, and a model of a ship in a glass bottle which reminded him of his mother. The sconce stayed in the shop for a very long time and was marked down again and again. No one knew how old he was, or where he came from.

He was eventually sold to a woman who wore a brocade dress every day with a suit jacket on top, and a gigantic plastic yellow rose in her hair.

She called herself Anastasia, and owned a restaurant. The restaurant was covered in decorative bric-à-brac, and the food was miserable and covered with red sauce, but very popular among bohemian and artistic sorts, including a famous eight-foot tall painter who carried a small tortoise around in his pocket and had, to the pride of the restaurant owner, given her a painting of the tortoise eating a plum. Anastasia felt she had an obligation to keep the eyes of her patrons stimulated. She continually added new things to her restaurant, searching through antique shops, the sales bins of department stores, and garbage bins. She carried a large basket with her everywhere, and a little box of tools including a hammer and a large pair of garden shears. She bought, stole, cut and stripped bits and bobs of the city as if it were her orchard: a forgotten public statue, a cupid on a gravestone rarely visited, a doorknocker shaped like a walrus, curtains in open windows, beautiful plants on windowsills, a bit of arabesque plaster off the façade of a building, the red accordion of a blind street musician, children's dolls and bears grabbed out of their hands as they napped on the metro, cats and birds which she would have taxidermied by a gentleman who gave her a discount as she brought him more animals than she could use herself.

In her restaurant there were peacock feathers, plastic lilies and flaking mannequin arms in vases, tin toys, devil and maiden marionettes that jiggled when the restaurant became busy, a plaster Venus, a large glass sculpture of a bulldog, a bronze Roman athlete, dented trumpets, a broken imitation Baroque harpsichord painted with pastoral scenes in which many rats lived, clocks, paper lanterns, beads, stuffed birds, cats, small dogs and white mice, parasols, lamps, music boxes and old jars of sausages, beets and pickles that would be lethal if opened. Hanging from the ceiling was a gigantic Harlequin made out of papier-mâché and cloth, and which, if shaken, would sprinkle those below with fleas, centipedes, maggots and ants. Everything was splattered with layers of red sauce and grease, which gave the fabrics, including the tablecloths and puppet clothes, a translucent quality. Anastasia's objects dutifully appeared in paintings, drawings, poems, films, and while she gave, she also took from her customers, quietly, like a mouse.

The kitchen wasn't important: an icebox, a filthy stove covered in pots filled with murky water in which everything was boiled, a stockpile of tinned red sauce, tinned duck, veal and pork, spaghetti in plastic packages, condensed milk, bottles of red wine vinegar, an old canvas sack full of yellow bread rolls, and a few mousetraps that hadn't been cleaned in years. The most important room in her restaurant was the archive, a former pantry filled with drawers and boxes in which she kept her patrons' paraphernalia. Stained napkins, photographs, broken teeth (she served her yellow bread rolls stale to encourage this), spectacles, hats, bowties, umbrellas, fingernails, earrings and other jewels. She kept a watchful eye, and underneath her dress on a long chain, a tiny pair of scissors she used to cut bits of their hair so slyly they never noticed. She also had a red leather journal for keeping track of who came when, what they ordered, and who they talked to. As she strolled around her restaurant during its busiest hours, kissing cheeks and upsetting plates with her brocaded body, her little hands were busy grabbing, pulling, picking up little treasures. Her prize possession was a mummified finger belonging to a painter who had committed suicide[2] and the emerald engagement ring of an opera singer. She sold the odd bit to a Brazilian or Japanese collector to keep herself in comfort, but nurtured the grand ambition of donating her collection to the state, or a museum, and being immortalized as a patron of the arts. Along with her objects, she kept a rotation of serving staff who

2   In the restaurant, the young painter, who was from Moldova, got into an argument with a bald Russian sculptor who cut off the painter's forefinger with a butter knife. It was a finger on the painter's left hand, the hand he painted with, and as it was pocketed by Anastasia before it could be found and sewn back on, he went back to his studio in despair, a hanky wrapped around the stump, and said to himself, 'Without the forefinger of my left hand, I might as well be without my —' and castrated himself. He bled to death from the wound. The whereabouts of his — was the obsession of Anastasia. It was rumoured to be hidden in an abstract bronze sculpture of a goat made by the Russian sculptor.

were all in one way or another, by her own judgement, beautiful, grotesque or exotic. One month she only employed dwarves and the next, only persons over six feet tall. When the sconce was hung in her restaurant, she only had women with facial disfigurements serving. She paid them horribly and pinched them.

Earwigs and cockroaches lived in the glass chandeliers hanging from the ceiling of her restaurant and mice chewed on the bread rolls before painters and critics did. The sconce did not mind such creatures and so he was happy, and in the restaurant he was reunited with the smell of his beloved rosemary, which was sprinkled in abundance on everything to hide rancidity.

A woman who hated fish came into the restaurant one night, not many weeks after the sconce arrived. She wore a black tuxedo and a hat shaped like a golden snail. She was accompanied by a young slim man with a drawn-on unibrow[3] who wore enormous amounts of perfume to try and drown out any sea smells in their vicinity.

The woman hated fish because her father had drowned in a shipwreck on its way to a far-off metropolis. She had nightmares about her father's body being eaten by fish and had spent a fortune on opiates, therapists and comforting luxuries to rid herself of it. She was an art critic. No artists had painted the sea, fish, whales, boats, oysters, or even glasses of water since her career had begun. Anastasia followed this rule: there were no signs

3   Without make-up, he had barely visible blond eyebrows but painted unibrows were very fashionable that season, and were called, for some strange reason, 'Doll's Fingers'. They were painted with either black, green or red make-up. The Doll's Fingers were, the next season, replaced with 'Doll's Moles', a painted dot above each eye rather than an eyebrow.

of marine life, no seafood, no sailors in the restaurant. Talk of sea voyages was strictly forbidden.

When her food came, the critic said, 'I did not order fish, I ordered pork chops with red sauce as I always do, and yet I smell fish. Did someone sneak fish into this dish?' She examined her pork chops then got out of her chair and sniffed around under tablecloths, by the tortoise painting, sniffed the other customers, their diseased genitals and legs, their cigarettes, and their meals, sniffed the disfigured faces of the waitresses, the toilets, and the carpets, until her nose landed on the sconce.

She demanded the sconce be taken off the wall.

'It stinks of the ocean, of fish, I feel seasick just looking at it.'

Anastasia hurriedly threw the sconce out and gave everyone a complimentary glass of red wine vinegar to calm their noses.

One of the waitresses took pity on the sconce and took him home along with her leftovers. She was very squat with a blonde bob and large red warts all over her face, which she covered with make-up when not working at Anastasia's restaurant. She lived above a shoe shop and had pictures all over her walls of a sad woman with a scar on her face and a little baby that looked like a sick old man.

She kissed the pictures of the scarred woman in the morning when she got home from work, and before bedtime. During the daytime, the sconce observed the pictures of the woman with the scarred face, which were covered in greasy lip prints, and enjoyed the scent of new shoes from the shop below.

The sconce could tell when the waitress started a job at a different restaurant: her smell went from red sauce and rats to clams and tobacco. Besides her leftovers, all she ate was cabbage, tea, and little sausages from a fancy looking tin.[4]

The waitress didn't see or talk to anyone. She picked at her warts, washed her clothes in a pot on the stove and listened to the radio. One night, she took the sconce off the wall, put candles in each of his cups, but rather than hanging him up again and lighting the candles, she brought him to bed, kissing his little face. The sconce enjoyed the sensation, and only wished that her mouth tasted like rosemary instead of clams and sausage. She took off her nightie, and tried out each candle, the sconce's face leaving an imprint on her thigh. The woman was a virgin and the candles were bloody when she pulled them out. She took them out of the sconce's bowls, and washed them in the bathroom before putting them back again.

The sconce continued to live in her bed. Sometimes mice and cockroaches crawled over him when the waitress wasn't there. One day, her breath stopped smelling like clams and she stopped leaving the apartment. She held the sconce to her breast. People knocked on her door and she didn't answer.

She left in the night, leaving all the pictures of the sad woman but one. She tried to fit the sconce into her purse but there wasn't room for two and she took the picture of the sad woman with scars instead.

Everything left in the apartment was thrown out, including the sconce. I don't know what will happen to it

4 There once was a woman who opened a tin of the same sausage brand to find a finger with the nail still on it. 'It can't be. It just looks like a finger, my eyes are deceptive, such a distinguished trusted brand would not allow fingers in their tins instead of sausages,' she said. She ate the finger as if it were a sausage and choked on the bone and died.

– it was found by an old man riding slowly around the city past midnight on a giant tricycle.[5]

5   The old man is missing one of his thumbs. When he was a child, he stuck his hand in the bathtub where his parents were keeping two large carp to eat for Christmas dinner. After getting stitches on the stump of his thumb, the boy's mother said she wouldn't cook the carp, they should be killed and buried. The father didn't want to waste them. When he sliced open their bellies, he removed their guts and the boy's mother had them buried in the family grave plot as she couldn't bear to throw chewed up bits of her son into the garbage. They ate the carp for Christmas dinner and the mother wept. The boy, for the rest of his life, could not eat fish without thinking about what those fish had eaten when alive...

.

EDWARD, DO NOT PAMPER THE DEAD

Bernadette worked in a variety shop, which had been a great appeal to Edward when he first met her. She worked in close proximity to cigarettes, chocolate bars and magazines with colour photographs, tinned cakes and green gumballs. Edward worked in an envelope-importing warehouse, as a clerk. Once, for Bernadette, he had stuck a small envelope in a larger envelope, on and on till he had used every kind of envelope he could find – it resembled a parcel. It would take a long time for Bernadette to open them all but he had forgotten to put a message inside the smallest envelope: the cleverness of his idea had excited him too much. When she got to the tiniest envelope, he grabbed it before she could open it, then asked her to move in with him. He had been thinking about it for a while, how comfortable it would be, how she would perhaps bring many goodies home from work.

On the day Bernadette was meant to move into the apartment Edward shared with his parents, Edward did not go home after work, but went to the movies to see *Pinocchio*, checking that it was accompanied by a piano instead of an organ, an instrument he hated. Original film sounds had gone missing somehow. He and Bernadette had seen *Dumbo* together. The film had been accompanied by an organ. The organ at the theatre was covered in bright paintings of birds, musical notes and fairy-tale characters, garish like a circus caravan or a chocolate box.

Edward thought the sound an organ made was like thin, wrinkly hands covered in fake, colourful jewels. They shared a box of multi-coloured, chalky candies Bernadette paid for, though she could have brought something more tasty from the store where she worked.

Edward's parents had sold all of their furniture to pay for his education. There were rectangular shadows all across the walls and floors where things used to be. It suited Edward remarkably fine, he hated furniture, and the thought of moving it. He had a recurring dream in which a large chest of drawers chased him down an endless staircase. With all the furniture gone the fear of his parents asking him to move it was gone too. Bernadette said she was bringing all the furniture from her mother's house, as her mother had recently died.

Bernadette lived in a shop front with her mother. The windows had red and green curtains, and were crowded with swan figurines. In the front garden, plastic flowers were shoved in the soil, they were very dirty and faded. In the centre was a painted concrete figurine of a duck wearing a sailor suit. There was a bit of sign left above the windows, it said 'PARSNIPS, MILK', making it easy for Edward to find his way there. The house next door scared Edward: the windowpanes were painted black and there was a chicken's foot nailed above the door.

Bernadette had two thin gold rings on her fingers. Edward did not know where they came from, nor did he add to them. Trinket jewels: they seemed a thing women were born with, even poor women.

Bernadette's mother had been the same shape as Bernadette, with a large bottom and a long neck, as if her body were a heavy pink gown hanging off her neck, or like an important civic building with a tall clock tower. She also had the same hair colour: a dark, rich red. She smelled sickly sweet. She would serve them minced crab, ungarnished, on tea saucers. There was only the one room in the house, and a bathroom. The room still had a long countertop and lots of shelves, left over from when it was a store, but the shelves were all empty except for some very thin red books and a tin with winged cupids and the word 'Sugar' on it. Bernadette and her mother slept on two pink velvet couches and cooked on a hotplate. How two such voluminous women could sleep comfortably on such hard, small couches and sustain their hunger with one hotplate, Edward did not know. It was better to sleep on no furniture at all, on the floor.

In the bathroom, there was a large box labelled 'RED ROSE POWDER HAIR DYE', and a block of soap the colour of butter. For wiping, there were strips of newspaper, cut evenly as if with scissors instead of ripped, as Edward's family did. He noticed all the strips were from ladies' newspapers. That must be what they read then, thought Edward. He cleaned himself with a strip advertising jelly moulds after emptying his bowels. The toilet wouldn't flush everything away, so he left it as it was.

When he arrived home after *Pinocchio*, Bernadette had moved in. He did not know how the furniture was moved in: he did not ask. His parents and Bernadette sat at the new, flimsy table Bernadette had brought, and ate tea, herrings and gherkins for dinner. Edward's parents looked like crumpled balls of newspaper and cloth.

Bernadette's two couches seemed even smaller and dirtier in his apartment, like two inedible prawns spat out by a disdainful and filthy mouth.

Edward was surprised to find, in the bedroom he now shared with Bernadette, that a large brass bedstead had replaced the pile of wool blankets and newspapers he had formerly slept on. The bed was covered with a bedspread made, he saw, with the green and red curtains from the room Bernadette had shared with her mother. He half expected to find the porcelain swans swimming about between them.

Bernadette wore flannel pyjamas to bed. He had imagined her owning long, high-collared nightgowns. Her legs looked like those of an elephant in the flannel trousers. The next day he bought her a long and garish green nightgown with a lacy, bib-type thing on the front, it was half see-through and the material made a sound when a hand was run across it. She wore it obediently. He took the flannel pyjamas for himself, tying them across his narrow waist with a bit of string. They were quite warm and comfortable.

When Edward's parents died, he and Bernadette were able to keep it quiet for five months that they were a couple living in a three-bedroom apartment, before the neighbourhood council assigned them two more people to live with.

Horace was twenty-two, but looked much older on account of his thick moustache, stomach, and ill-fitting brown suits, plus the wart on his cheek with a hair growing from it that he never shaved, and a lack of rosy youthfulness in his jowls. There was always some bit of savoury sauce on his face, always a bit of his white underpants sticking through his open fly, always a faecal smell about his person. Whatever he did, he made enough money to be able to buy fried mutton, and newspapers.

The Child played piano in the cinema. She didn't really know how to play the piano; she knew how to play two songs, and couldn't read music. The songs she knew were 'The Wedding of the Painted Doll' and 'Animal Crackers in My Soup'. She could get by playing those two songs for hundreds of movies. She wore a black suit to work. Her hair was frizzy blonde. All the Child brought for her room was a rickety ironing board, on which she slept with a scraggly patchwork quilt made of dull colours, and a hand-tinted postcard of Rudolph Valentino, so that he had red lips, very pink skin and a green suit. She stuck it above the ironing board.

Horace brought a poster of a cartoon sardine with very long eyelashes wearing a clam-shell brassiere and a short skirt, lounging by the seaside. He had wanted to put it in the bathroom, but Bernadette did not allow it. He put it up in his room. Across his window, instead of a curtain, he taped a black and white picture of children riding on a carousel, torn badly from a newspaper. He spent most of his money on the newspapers, and bought them all, so that there were stacks and stacks in his room, but he would not let the others use them for toilet wiping, in case he wanted to reread them. Above his bed there were rows of dried boogers stuck to the wall.

Bernadette bought more things for her and Edward's room. A picture of an Arthur Rackham fairy on the wall. A small dark wood wardrobe, in which Edward made Bernadette keep her mirror. Also inside were suits for Edward, five dresses belonging to Bernadette, a hat box full of underthings and socks, and an extra pair of shoes – Mary Janes with quite a tall heel.

Behind all the clothes, wrapped in newspaper, was a portrait of Bernadette done in charcoal by an old school friend of Edward's. Edward couldn't remember much of that friend, except that he wore a beige suit with a loose blue bowtie, that his hair was long, and that he had taken a train to live somewhere else. He sent them a postcard once. The light blue ink on the back was too damaged and lightened from travelling for them to discern what it said, and the postcard was later lost.

On top of the wardrobe was a cardboard box with hearts on it full of needles, buttons, metal thimbles, a Chinese pincushion, thread, whatnot, and a wad of cash and coins, Bernadette's savings. The box was from Bernadette's work, it had once held red-foil-covered chocolate hearts.

'There were none for us to have, of course,' Edward often said, lifting the box to his nose to smell the remnants of chocolate. Beside the chocolate box was something that disturbed Edward greatly: a sewing machine catalogue. Some of the machines were circled in blue ink. Bernadette's plan was to save up for a sewing machine so she could work from home and have a child. They couldn't afford a child on Edward's salary alone. Bernadette said her friend Margaret sewed men's trousers and had three children now. Edward had never met Margaret, it seemed a surprise that Bernadette should have other acquaintances besides himself, he felt like Margaret was made up.

Slipped inside the catalogue was a list of names on a scrap of pink envelope:

Edward Little
Paul
Susan
~~Joyce~~
Beatrice
Louisa
Jane
Juniper
Wilbur

The 'Edward Little' frightened him as much as his reflection, Edward-in-the-Mirror, did. He took coins when he could from Bernadette's pile, to prevent Edward Little/ Wilbur/Jane as best he could.

He never added to it. Never.

128

One baby and they could be rid of Horace, two and the Child would have to go too – but first the machine, or else they wouldn't be able to afford it, Bernadette said. She wanted her baby.

There was the Child, wasn't she good enough, said Edward, wouldn't she do? He had dreamt of the sewing machine many times, he was convinced Bernadette and the machine would somehow become one being, a silver needle coming out of Bernadette's mouth where her teeth should have been. In his dreams, he lay flat on her lap, and she sewed his hands to his feet and so forth. Her neck bent her face almost touching her thighs, but for Edward in-between.

Edward was worried that Horace would interfere with the Child, that was a great enough responsibility. Horace once said to Edward, of the Child: 'She got no hairs on.' Horace told Edward he had a number of girlfriends, and that he sodomized them, it was the only clever way to do a woman, he said. Edward followed his advice, though it made Bernadette weep.

The bathroom had a large, long skylight, it was horrifically cold. Edward hated to use it, and so kept a chamber pot underneath the bed. He often said out loud that he would be more inclined to bathe if he had a fur coat to slip into afterwards. Yes, he dreamed of someday owning a long, brown fur coat, to wear over his suit. He would no longer sleep in the bed, but simply take off his coat wherever and lie down on it. He would sew treats into the lining (peanuts, gum, playing cards, toffee) and cut them out in the middle of the night when no one else was awake using a tiny pair of scissors no one else would know about, and he would keep them under the loose floorboard in the hall which was his secret. Ideally, Bernadette would use her sewing machine savings to buy him the coat, it was the only way he could ever have one. The last Christmas she had been frugal, she was saving her money for the machine, and gave Edward the same gifts she gave to Horace and the Child: boxes of cherry-flavoured chocolates, and boxes of cigarettes.

For Bernadette, he had bought a side of bacon and a kettle and for Horace, a box of liquorice wheels and a toy pocket watch, a piece of thin metal with a paper face and hands that didn't move on it. Horace was greatly impressed, real watches were the most expensive thing, a fake one gave him a feeling of status, though it told him nothing. Fake clocks and pocket watches were sold everywhere, cheap popular things, most children had fake pocket watches like Horace, who put his in his suit pocket and often pretended to check the time on it with such seriousness Edward could not laugh at him. He deeply regretted the liquorice, as it turned Horace's spittle and boogers a dark brown. The dried snot on his wall looked like crushed flies.

Edward had bought the Child a set of paper dolls for Christmas. She didn't dress them, but put each individual piece up on her wall, like a wallpaper design, surrounding Rudolph with hats, trousers and people in their underwear. Horace bought her a toy piano. He didn't buy anyone else a present, not even Bernadette. It was an upright white plastic children's piano with colourful music notes and birds painted on the sides. Whichever key you pressed, it played 'Pop Goes the Weasel'.

Edward became fearful that the piano would attract tiny men the way a piece of cheese left on a countertop attracted mice, or perhaps even that a tiny man lived inside it and would come out at night. He went out to buy rodenticide. There was a risk the Child would eat the rodenticide and become sick, he knew, but he had to distribute it around the apartment. He knew of an exterminator's shop, with a bright pink sign. The exterminator's children were covered in scratches, and drooled. One of them wore a small square cage over its head. They hung around outside the shop, using brooms to beat the dead rats, pigeons and raccoons nailed across the shop front. Beside the exterminator's shop there was a bakery, the window display a row of green and pink blancmange. Edward bought himself a pink blancmange, which they wrapped in newspaper, and tied with string. It was covered in grey marks when he unwrapped it. He ate the whole thing in his and Bernadette's bedroom with the door closed, he did not want to share it.

The box the rat poison came in wasn't well made, it had left a fine dust of poison on Edward's fingers, and of course he did not use a spoon to eat the blancmange, but sat it on his lap and scooped handfuls into his mouth. Bernadette had to feed him a mixture of baking soda and vinegar when he showed signs of poisoning. The blancmange came up like bits of organs no one ever hoped to see, pink and gelatinous. The sight of Edward throwing up in the kitchen made the Child also throw up, thick yellow spittle, three black buttons and a penny.

Edward retired to bed and stayed there longer than necessary.

When he was better, he wrapped the piano up with newspaper and string, put it in a bag and threw it into a canal. Bernadette cleaned up all the poison.

The note was delivered to Bernadette at eleven fifteen the next morning. She had been at work since eight, in the variety store. It was a Sunday, and she had sold a great deal of cigarettes.

She paid the post person, shuttered the shop, and told
her superior, who was unpacking boxes of mint cakes
in the storage room, that she must leave immediately, as
something dreadful had happened to her Edward.

Edward lay on the floor beside their bed, half covered
by a blanket. He blinked when he saw Bernadette.

'Bernadette,' he said, 'I have died.'

It was true.

Bernadette wept for a while, sitting on the bed, before
leaving the apartment to use a telephone to make the funeral arrangements and find a church where he could
lie. An ash-coloured suit was purchased at Edward's
request, and flowers, and food.

The Child and Horace did not know what to do. The
Child cried, while Horace said, over and over again, 'A
shame'.

The Child was not a child, she was just small. She
was older than Edward, Bernadette and Horace, but
kept this to herself, and cried in a most childish manner
when Edward said he had died.

Edward did not cry during his own funeral, but
blinked solemnly. His glasses were folded and placed
in his jacket collar, but he did not really need them, he
could see perfectly fine.

The Child wore her black suit, and Horace wore a
brownish green one he must have purchased for the funeral. Edward had never seen it before, but it certainly
was not appropriate for such a serious, sad event – he
even had a bright blue kerchief in the top pocket.

On a table there was a small marbled pound cake,
a bowl of foil-covered chocolates, some white bread

132

spread with margarine, and sardines arranged in circles with their tails all meeting in the middle, so they looked like silver flowers. Edward recognized the food, they were all things that could be bought in the shop where Bernadette worked. Bernadette made him up a plate and brought it to him as he was meant to be lying down in the coffin the whole time.

He hadn't asked them to line his coffin with fur, and felt a melancholic pride in his own economy. He had always wanted a fur coat, and now he would never have one.

He put one of the sardines and two of the chocolates from his plate behind his coffin pillow to have for later. All in black, Bernadette resembled a sombre funeral carriage. Her veil was made from a bit of sheer black stocking. She has ruined a pair of stockings to mourn me, thought Edward to himself, and felt loved.

Bernadette visited him every day after work in the church he was placed in. She brought him two slices of toast with mustard spread on them, his thermos once again filled with tea, and an egg when she could spare it.

Edward often sent notes to Bernadette such as:

BRING ME BOILED EGGS AND A THERMOS OF TEA
PLEASE MY DARLING

When she visited him, Bernadette could see Edward's large nose and his long thin hands holding a cigarette, poking out of the coffin as soon as she walked into the church basement, where his coffin was, along with many others. There were large boxes of cigarettes, newspapers hanging on sticks, plain toast, a large tea urn full of lukewarm, weak tea. That's all they were provided with.

'The newspapers we get are a few days behind, they

133

are donated by charitable persons, I have read them all,' Edward told Bernadette, hinting that she could bring him one of the magazines with coloured photos from her shop.

In the coffin next to his lay a pregnant woman. Her face was covered in warts, her hair was very greasy and cut short, like an upside down brown bowl. Her stomach was very prominent and firm, there were spots on her shirt where her nipples lay.

'The poor baby, to be born dead,' Bernadette whispered to Edward, and pressed her veil against her cheek to dry the tears that formed. Edward was silent, for he hadn't noticed the pregnant woman before.

'Will you fetch me a newspaper from the counter Bernadette, preferably a fresher one?'

When she returned with the paper in hand, Edward placed it over his head, like a small tent.

'Tomorrow, may you bring me some fish and toffee Bernadette?' he said, and said no more. She left, sobbing.

In the church basement where Edward lay, there was a sign made with embroidery that said

DO NOT PAMPER THE DEAD

Most of the dead were elderly people who wet their coffins and spat into the newspapers, as they didn't have hankies.

The Child visited him just once. She told Edward that she thought her eyes were ruined. Valentino was just a blur of green and grey now, and would he give her some advice on purchasing glasses? Edward advised her against it, saying glasses were unflattering for a woman – he'd hate to see her wear them – and difficult to maintain, they needed to be polished all the time and so forth.

He wagged a long finger at her.

'Do not come here by yourself again. Remember you are a vulnerable person.'

The Child obeyed. She did not come again, though he missed her.

The last time Bernadette went to visit Edward, she was wearing a pair of men's boots. Her stocking veil had runs in it, she had not cut herself a new one. He could see little sores all around her mouth.

She would quit her job at the variety store soon, she said, as she was pregnant. The Child had moved in with an organ player from another cinema. The baby was Horace's.

Ah, with small movements of her thighs and hips, a finger slipped from one orifice to the other, she had managed to procure a pregnancy out of Horace, thought Edward. He was paying for half of the sewing machine, it was being delivered later that day, said Bernadette. She would sew nightgowns.

'With the baby, they won't move anyone else into the house, it will be just like it was when you were young and lived with your father and mother,' she said. 'Now, goodbye, Edward. I won't have time to visit you.'

HUNGARIAN SPRATS

On his first voyage to Europe, Baron Dąmbski had lost his monogrammed leather luggage and all it contained. He was not a Baron, just as his younger brother was not a Count, and his older brother not a Prince, but those were the first names their wealthy industrialist father had given them. His monogram was an intertwined B and D contained in a diamond shape.

Many of his belongings, including the lost suitcases, were made in Europe. The movement of products back and forth over the oceans gave him a great feeling of anxiety, and every night since the loss of his luggage, he had dreamt of being on a sinking ship stuffed with delicious, alluring things, not knowing what to save. The dream ended with him floating on an Italian Mannerist painting of a long-necked woman, surrounded by whales and octopuses laughing at him.

The humiliating loss of his possessions and his beloved luggage prevented him from returning to Europe, though he longed for it. One morning, while struggling to open a can of oysters, he hurt his hand with his golden can opener. 'Impossible to open without great strain!' he said to himself, and called one of his servants who managed, with some effort, and the bleeding of his fingers, to open the can with a large knife. 'How safe my possessions would be from thieves if they were in a can!' Baron exclaimed.

The canning factory he approached with his idea, the Hungarian Food Company Inc., was owned by a friend of his father. The owner was not Hungarian and nor were his products, but he wanted to evoke the glory of Budapest and the confusion people often had between Hungary and hungry. Behind his desk was a poster of a can with a label depicting a globe on it. Above the can were the words

CAN THE WHOLE WORLD

The factory canned: asparagus, turtles, oysters, mushrooms, water chestnuts, clams, peas, herrings, sardines, snails, peaches, oysters, ham, anchovies, tuna, eggplant, salmon, white beans, mussels, caviar, pearl onions, pears, rice wrapped in grape leaves, gherkins, pigeon, peppers, bamboo shoots, octopus, pineapple, crab, artichoke hearts, pig hearts, calf hearts, chicken hearts, beets, beef, sausages, apples, duck, corn, livers, carrots, pineapple, soups of all kinds, custard, goat meat, mutton.

Canning whole calves and turkeys proved to be disastrous, as the meat was too large, the can too big for everything to be cooked and preserved. Canning a whole chicken or a whole piglet in jelly proved very successful.

The owner of the Hungarian Food Company Inc. wanted to move beyond food, to take in all the world's chaos, and to spit it out again in uniform shapes. He created a line of novelty toy cans with jack-in-the-box-like spring clowns inside of them instead of food, sold in joke stores.

Perhaps Baron's idea could catch on. Secure and dis-creet luggage, secretive storage – no thief would steal a dented can of sprats, would they? Thus all of Baron's possessions were canned in sizes ranging up to five pounds, and for extra security, labelled 'sprats'. Out of vanity, Baron had a well-known graphic artist design a label in the style fashionable at the time, a nude faun grappling with a fish.

In his enthusiasm he did not think that he would need anything on the long voyage itself, his cans packed below deck. His beard grew long, he did not take his fur coat off, and he was rumoured to be an exotic animal from Central America on its way to a European zoo. Baron's servant, Otto, had in his modest pigskin suitcase the following: a package of dried apricots, three pairs of underpants, the complete short stories of Tolstoy, a can opener, a razor blade, an extra pair of trousers, a pair of grey socks, and an Italian dictionary. Baron was too proud to borrow the razor or underpants. His clothes were sent to the ship's laundry facilities daily, and as they were being cleaned, he wandered the ship with his fur coat held firmly shut.

Otto spent the voyage in dreadful anticipation of having to utilize the can opener hundreds of times under Baron's gaze in the suite of a London hotel. Baron planned to have his possessions recanned before heading to the continent, and again before heading home. The canning factory in his home country had factory contacts all over Europe, cousins of his – they would discreetly and securely bring his possessions to their factories, where they already had the labels made. Baron had paid them in advance. The Hungarian Food Company Inc. had contacts all over Europe and Baron had limitless pockets.

Baron waited at his hotel. His metallic luggage, packed in boxes, did not arrive. Instead, through some miscommunication, the boxes of 'sprats' were brought to a warehouse, and from there distributed all over Europe for consumption.

Baron thought to take out newspaper ads calling for the return of all cans, but Otto advised him against it considering the many discreet items within. All over

Europe, people opened cans, expecting to find fish, but instead finding the following: a single hanky, a container of liquorice-flavoured lozenges, silver shirt cuffs, a pocket English-German dictionary, a pocket Polish-Italian dictionary, a pair of opera glasses, silk underpants, a pipe, a set of erotic cards depicting women with exotic animals (lion, elephant, etc), a single shoe, a tangle of black suspenders which the opener first thought were eels, a box of lambskin condoms, reading spectacles, small golden scissors shaped like a heron, large silver scissors, an eighteenth-century Harlequin figurine, a maroon celluloid dildo, twenty white dress shirts, all in their own cans, which resembled ghosts when pulled out, causing at least five nervous attacks and one death, a bottle of hair oil, a shoe horn, a glass bottle shaped like a coiled snake full of an amber-smelling cologne, tweezers, a toy hippo made out of leather, an umbrella, six fountain pens, cream-coloured envelopes tied together with ribbon, sixty sheets of Italian marbled paper, eighty sheets of plain cream paper, a paper knife, a stamp container, a silver and lacquer cigarette case, an ivory ashtray shaped like a swan, a comb, a large silver-backed brush, a small silver-backed brush, a hand mirror, an empty powder jar, a powder puff, a pair of black silk socks (a hundred cans), a pair of mustard-coloured socks, a pair of white socks, a pair of blue socks, a pair of salmon-pink socks, a red rubber and brass enema syringe, a pot of anise-flavoured toothpaste, a cane that folded into three parts, a sewing kit, a tin of buttons, including ivory buttons, gold buttons and black satin-covered buttons, a retractable gold and ivory back-scratcher in the shape of a dainty hand, a cream waistcoat, a black waistcoat (six cans of each), one pin-stripe waistcoat, a black jacket (there were twelve such cans), one tweed jacket, one pinstripe jacket, a pair of black trousers (there were thirty cans of trousers altogether), a pair of pinstripe trousers, a pair of tweed trousers, a soap box with a bar of purple soap inside, a manicure set, a gold matchbox, a pair of black finished binoculars, an oriental silk robe, a pair of white gloves, a pair of brown gloves, a pair of grey gloves, a pair of black gloves, a glove stretcher, a toothbrush in a silver case, a corkscrew, a stiff-bristled clothes brush, a curling iron, an ivory and gilded metal snuff box, a map of Europe, a guide to hotels in London, a hat made out of beaver, a shaving kit, six white bowties, seven black bowties, a paisley bowtie, a red bowtie, an oyster fork, a green wooden mask from Central America with a spider on its nose – the spiders' legs spreading out across the cheeks like a moustache, the mask was too small for the wide face of Baron so it was purely decorative – a lacquered fold-out shaving mirror, a copper percolator, shoe polish, a beige rubber ball, a ragged topsy-turvy doll, one half with white skin, the other with black, a pistol, a striped knitted cotton swimsuit, a leather-bound edition of *The Diary of Countess Françoise Krasinska, written in the final years of the reign of King Augustus III* by Klementyna Hoffmanowa, a mahogany stereoscope fitted with a double image of a ballerina, a polished circle of amber with an insect inside, a small table clock, a silver pocket watch, a yellow towel, a green wool blanket, a single slipper (there were six such cans), a magnifying glass, a small rose-coloured pillow, a taxidermied black North American squirrel, a watercolour paint set, twenty small cut squares of watercolour paper, a small black leather notebook with thick paper, a pair of leather and canvas sports boots, a bowler hat, a trilby hat, a straw boater hat, a white cotton vest, a pair of leather mules, a jumper with horn buttons, a black overcoat with a beige fur lining, a dinner jacket (fifteen cans altogether, two per can), a knitted jumper, a peaked cap, a pair of leather sandals, purple silk pyjamas, green silk pyjamas, yellow silk pyjamas, a large cotton nightgown, a bottle of iron tablets, eighteen tie pins and, finally, a tin of oysters, of a much higher grade than those produced by the Hungarian Food Company Inc.

Baron was able to recover: a photograph of himself as a boy dressed as a peasant, a glass bottle of witch-hazel, a Vienna bronze bear whose stomach contained a compartment holding digestive tablets he had bought in preparation for the gastric novelties of European restaurants, and an extremely delicate and realistic cupid made out of coloured beeswax in a glass, coffin-shaped box. He returned home with each remaining possession taped to his chest underneath his fur coat, and never left again.

THE MOTH EMPORIUM

It had been five years since I went into the costume shop. It was only a few blocks away from my mother's house, but I always hurried my pace when I walked by it. It was in a converted Victorian house, the exterior was painted gold, turquoise and black, like a cartoon version of an Egyptian tomb. In the window, between two sides of a thick purple curtain, a mannequin wearing an eighteenth-century wig with devil horns, gold snake-shaped jewellery and a black lacy dress held a sign that said

COSTUMES, VINTAGE AND UNIQUE FINDS

The shop was surrounded by a fence of dismembered mannequin limbs painted blue. They were female limbs, slim, ideal ones so unlike my own that to see them, even out of the corner of my eye, made me self-conscious. If the weather was nice, there were clothes outside, racks of coats and dresses, colourful bins of scarves and rows of cowboy boots, as if the owners had been forced to take them off before entering, never to return. The upmost window, belonging to the attic, was covered with a poster of a grinning turn-of-the-century moon.

The shop was both tempting and sickening, like a gingerbread house. It was owned by a horrible couple – two immense Germans with blonde hair. They looked like they ate a lot of sausages. Their faces, their hands, seemed larger than most. The man dressed in black Oxford shirts, black jeans and black leather vests – he could've been mistaken for a pastor, if you squinted and did not notice his black snakeskin boots and the sinister rings which covered his knuckles like gold and silver warts. He resembled, if such a thing existed, a male witch. The woman wore lots of leather, and black stock-ings with complex patterns on them. Her make-up was always blue, beige, red, and around her wide waist was a belt made out of bullets.

I had only been inside once. My younger sister had wanted a mask. I was seventeen and she was fifteen at the time. We never went to costume shops because our mother made most of our costumes, skeletons, moons, witches, ladybirds. But a mask was beyond our moth-er's skill – the papier-mâché one she had made, using water and flour, hadn't dried properly and became mil-dewed. My sister and I both had dark brown hair like our mother. My sister had acne scars, but she was so pretty, it looked like decoration on her face. If anyone needed a mask, it was me. My face looked like that of a very thin elephant, large ears and nose, small eyes. I hat-ed wearing costumes, I hadn't done so since I was eight: I believed I was so ugly, I couldn't disguise myself as anything else. The shop smelled like nag champa, moth-balls and face make-up. There were wings, white, red, black, pink, made out of chicken feathers, plastic noses, piles of Russian navy shirts and knitwear from north-ern countries, gowns, boas, leather jackets, top hats, frills, ribbons, shoes, corsets, such variety of segments, pieces, slices, scraps, strips, it was hard not to think of a butcher's shop.

There were crinolines, like multi-coloured clouds seemingly floating across the ceiling of the shop, but which in fact dangled off hooks. There was no one in the shop when we went in, only a plaster Elvis bust on the countertop, a female mannequin with a beehive wig, and a male mannequin in a giant gold birdcage wearing a green-feathered outfit.

At the back of the shop was the wall of masks, wood,

rubber, leather, Venetian, Mexican, Indonesian. The rubber ones were the most frightening because they were misshapen without heads wearing them, like flayed skin. I thought I saw the eyes of a mask move, but the floorboards of the shop were so uneven, the wares so overwhelming, it must have been a trick. My sister went towards them, and grabbed a grey wolf mask made out of wood, holding it against her face, and howling.

I looked at the crinolines. There was one that was grey, like a pouf of smoke escaped from a train in which one could disappear. With my sister's encouragement I pulled it down and went into a changing room while she went to look at the masks. I put the crinoline over my clothes, but it looked messy – like I was a doll covered in cobwebs pulled out of an attic – so I took off everything I was wearing, even my bra, my stockings and under-wear. I put the crinoline back on, and looked at myself, unexpectedly entranced in the changing room mirror. We didn't have a full-length mirror at home – you had to stand on the toilet to look at yourself in the small round mirror above the sink.

Behind me, there was no longer a curtain, but a glaring, toad-like face and a black, religious-looking hat. I turned around, covering my breasts with my hands. He closed the curtain again.

I hurriedly put my clothes back on and stepped out, leaving the crinoline in the changing room. He was waiting there, his arms crossed. He pointed to a sign which read

PLEASE ASK BEFORE USING THE CHANGING ROOMS

My sister, watching us, dropped the mask. It broke into three pieces.

The woman appeared out of nowhere, screaming at her that the mask cost three hundred dollars and we would have to pay for it. My sister ran past her, and grabbed my wrists. We ran out together.

They didn't follow us out – I don't know why, perhaps there was a law against chasing children. They must have been watching us on a security camera, said my sister. We laughed, and laughed, out of fear.

After that, whenever we broke something around the house my sister would scream in a fake German accent. It had become funny to us, but still – we never went back inside the shop, and avoided walking past it.

.

When I returned, those years later, the costume shop looked gloomier than I remembered it, the clothes on the racks appropriate for scarecrows, the colourful paint flaking, the moon poster covering the attic window wrinkled like a grape. There was a sign that said

2 FOR 1 CASHMERE

– that was what drew me in. They surely wouldn't remember me, I was almost twenty-two.

I had gone away to university, while my sister had stayed home. She chose the same art college our mother went to, only fifteen minutes away by bicycle. I went to a small university in a small town, with nice old stone buildings and very cold weather – it was on a lake and one felt the cold lake wind even in the library. I studied Scandinavian literature, so the setting suited me. I never had the money to go on an exchange to anywhere in Scandinavia, or even visit. My specialization was

Danish literature, I could read very well, and write, in Danish. I wasn't Danish myself, but I had learned about Denmark as a child through blue tins of butter biscuits, and Hans Christian Andersen. I was writing a novel in Danish. One of the characters was a beautiful door knob who moved through various houses and apartments, that's all I'll say. I received a rejection letter from a Danish literary magazine, for a short story. They had written back to me in Danish though I didn't have a Danish name, which I was proud of.

After graduating I had nowhere to go but home. I hadn't found a job yet, though my sister worked part-time in a shop selling tea and crystals. She painted very small pictures of foxes, bears and other woodland creatures having tea parties among the trees; if you looked closely you could see the contents of the teacups were red, and if you looked even closer, you could see a little girl's shoe or ribbon somewhere in the painting, hiding in the grass or hanging from a branch. Our mother was an artist too: she taught art at a Russian private school. Under her instruction they mostly painted pictures of horses and copied Andrei Rublev icons.

Since I was thirteen I had always worn the same outfit: drab brown skirts and black sweaters from the Salvation Army. I wanted to think about clothes very little, and be noticed as little as possible. In the shop again, I chose two black jumpers, but didn't try them on: one seemed very large, the other small, but I didn't care. To my relief, there was a pale and sour-looking young man with a blue Mohawk behind the counter instead of the Germans. He wore a pinstripe suit with a waistcoat and a spiky dog collar. He rang my sweaters through without looking at me and put them in a bright yellow and red bag which I stuffed in my purse as soon as I was outside, standing on the steps. I didn't like colours, and I didn't want my sister to know where I had been.

He was there, the German owner, crouching – he was repainting one of the legs, with a tiny bucket of blue. He stood up when he saw me, so suddenly that I jumped, and asked if I wanted a job. His name was Wolf.

I thought that he wanted me to work to pay for the mask my sister had broken, but he didn't seem to remember who I was. Instead he told me he paid above minimum wage, that it wasn't a difficult job, that he really needed help, it was only him and the young man, Raven, inside. He didn't ask whether I took an interest in fashion (I didn't) or knew how to sew or use a till. I said yes, to the job, I didn't have any other opportunities, besides my Danish novel, but I wouldn't have if it didn't seem like the German woman was gone. I looked up at the store, at its windows, for her face. There was only the moon, like a death mask.

It was easiest to sell the clothes that were second-hand as people couldn't ask for different sizes and we didn't bear much responsibility for the personality of the clothes, how they were made and looked. They were simply passing through us, as if we were a train or a steamship. Wolf washed and patched them up but made no drastic changes. Also easy were the cheap costumes that came in plastic packages: Frankenstein, witches, nurses, they couldn't be returned if opened. The imitation eighteenth-century garments made me nervous, they were soft and difficult contraptions, heavy as bodies themselves. There were drawers full of buttons shaped like moons and *Alice in Wonderland* characters, and drawers full of ties, cufflinks and garter belts. The countertops were glass, and filled with rings, brooches and necklaces. Earrings hung from a string above the counter like tiny clothes on a laundry line. Behind the counter, Wolf kept a bottle of castor oil in case anyone tried on a ring too small – the oil helped slide it off.

I brought a notebook with me to the shop and made lists of clothes to use in my Danish novel: braided military coats, plastic Viking hats, neckties, striped stockings, white ruffs, long blue dresses.

There was an old computer underneath the counter that played songs in a continual loop: April Stevens, Patsy Cline, The Beach Boys, 'The Monster Mash', the *Rocky Horror Picture Show* soundtrack, Dion and the Belmonts, and other music typical for a costume shop. I longed for Schubert, Schumann, and string quartets by Tchaikovsky. I played them on my music player when no one else was there, hooking it up to the speakers.

Backstage, there was an elaborate amount of traps and poison to keep vermin away, moths, rats and mice. The costume shop was between a Chinese shop selling eggs and tofu and a natural foods bakery, so there were always rats around. We burned nag champa to cover the smell of mothballs. I hated disposing of used rodent traps. We also sold oversized rat and mice costumes – ears, long rubber tails.

I hated the fur coats, which hung like giants' beards, and the saucy people who came in and bought them, men with moustaches and female models who looked like long, bony fingers, or insects.

I sometimes dreamt that I put one of the coats on and Isak Dinesen mistook me for a lion and chased me around the shop, trying to shoot me.

.

I watched Wolf closely. His face reminded me of a bust

of Beethoven I had seen at university. He wore the following rings: one of the glass eyeball rings that were popular sellers in the shop, a silver ring shaped like an eagle, a gold ring with a hunk of amber, another gold one with a tiny circle of ruby, and another silver ring shaped like a wolf's head. He was very tall, with a large belly. He wore the same things every day, like me, his uniform of black trousers, a black vest and a white shirt. The only thing that changed was his hat, but each was made out of black felt, as if it was the same hat shapeshifting according to his mood. A black bowler, a black tyrolean hat with a black feather on its brim, a capello like a Catholic clergyman. The rare times he wasn't wearing a hat, his hair was white, and combed in an old-fashioned manner with oil I imagined was popular when he was a boy. On his vest he often wore a gold brooch in the shape of an elephant's head.

There was something creaky about him, I wondered if he had a wooden leg, a glass eyeball, a piece of metal somewhere inside his body holding things together, a fake tooth, an organ that once belonged to someone else.

Raven wasn't happy I was given the job. He had been working there since before Eule – that was her name – died, and was made full-time when she became ill. He told me when Wolf wasn't there. Raven was older than I originally thought. He was like an antique porcelain figurine of a child with cracks in it. He talked about Eule with admiration, a lot, about how she threw wild costume parties, had interesting tattoos all over her body. He talked about her so much that I had a dream I found a mask of her face at the back of the shop. It screamed at me with its big red mouth, and I threw it against the wall. It broke into pieces, but still screamed, the bits of mouth splitting into their own voices, a choir of screechy

152

German.

Wolf was going for periods of time, from days to a few weeks, leaving Raven and me to run the shop. He was buying things around the world to sell in the shop from milliners in Switzerland, jewellery-makers in Morocco, mask-makers in southern Germany. That's why the shop wasn't like anywhere else, though he wasn't above plastic stuff made in China – we sold that too. Wolf left and returned wearing a great, long overcoat, and carrying a shabby-looking olive military knapsack. He was followed a few weeks later by crates and boxes.

I made a lot of mistakes. I rolled an expensive Edwardian dress into a messy ball and stuffed it into a plastic shopping bag. I also put a top hat awkwardly into a bag though there were special hat boxes for them to be carried in. I spilled a box of fake pearls which rolled into the wide cracks of the floorboards and had to be cleaned up with a vacuum. Wolf split the vacuum bag with a knife like an animal's belly and emptied the pearls into a jar, but didn't give me a harsh word, let alone fire me.

He never yelled, and he was never angry. When I told him I studied Danish and planned on being a Danish novelist he laughed at me, not in a cruel way, and told me he would help me to learn German too, it wouldn't be so hard if I already knew Danish.

He lived above the shop alone, on the top three floors. He sometimes invited me upstairs, before and after work, for black coffee and black bread, or apple pancakes. His apartment looked like a continuation of the shop, mannequin heads, boxes full of wigs and shoes, great piles of fashion books – the kind of books that seemed like useless, colossal monsters in comparison to the ones I loved. The walls were covered in pictures, probably cut out from magazines, and even books. He had Sid Vicious,

Pee-wee Herman, David Bowie, Siouxsie Sioux, Elvis, Marc Bolan, Twiggy, Andy Warhol – people like that, whose height of fame and sometimes death happened before I was born, but not too far in the past to interest me. There was also a large poster of Betty Boop, posters for the films *Pink Flamingos*, *The Bride of Frankenstein* and *Dracula*, and a cartoonish painting of a sausage with a smiling face. One wall was covered in halves of doll faces. The ones with eyelids batted their eyelashes when you walked by, as the floor was so creaky.

The kitchen was filthy, the cupboards and stove were covered in grease the colour of earwigs, but one hardly noticed at first because of all the interesting stuff: a bowl full of plastic fruit with faces – the apple had buckteeth, the banana leopard spots and fangs; a Felix the Cat teapot; Frida Kahlo pin-up girls and cartoon animal fridge magnets; the colourful cans of fish soup I expected would never be opened, they had rust along their rims. The bottom half of the kitchen window was obscured by enormous glass jars full of pickles with bits of garlic and dill dancing around inside. On the table was a wooden incense smoker shaped like a shepherd with a long beard, holding a pipe, and a nutcracker wearing a hussar coat.

It happened on a slow day in the shop. It was raining outside and I had to rush to take everything in, the racks and shoes now crowding the front of the shop made it hard to navigate. I grabbed one of the braided military jackets, royal blue with gold, and slipped into a changing room. In that moment I imagined wearing it in my Danish author photo, like some sort of Hamlet. As I had years before, I took off almost everything before putting on the coat, and like years before, he appeared out of nowhere, opening the curtain. Instead of screaming, I turned around, and grabbing him by the shirt, pulled him in with me.

.

For our wedding, Wolf wore the same clothes he wore every day. He told me to choose anything I wanted from the shop. There were piles of wedding dresses, the kind girls purchased to wear at Hallowe'en, their faces painted to resemble corpses. I felt like a fool, a bride in a costume shop. I borrowed money from the till and bought a smart, dark blue dress suit, brand new, from a department store, with large buttons, and a matching hat, stockings and shoes. It didn't look how I wanted to look. I resembled an air stewardess, like I was wearing a costume, though that was exactly what I wanted to avoid.

My mother wore her best dress, a green sagging antique thing from the 1920s with a very old, faded peacock feather sewn onto a sash that was yellow like an old band aid, and a black flowered shawl. My sister wore red Ukrainian dancing boots, and a pink frock with a lace Peter Pan collar. I was relieved she didn't bring one of her cruel, thin boyfriends from art college who, like Raven, gave me dirty looks for not being beautiful. Wolf didn't invite any family, I don't think he had any besides a few cousins in Germany. He did invite an Italian man with a ducktail who bought lots of jewellery for himself at Wolf's shop.

I saw Wolf's age on our marriage certificate for the first time. He was fifty-four years old.

As a wedding present my sister gave me a small painting of Little Red Riding Hood and the Wolf in bed together. It was painted on wood, medieval in style, the figures stiff and flat-looking, but with wonderful detail.

For our wedding feast we had cold cuts, black bread, spice cake, and champagne above the shop. Wolf sat me on his lap, to the discomfort of my mother and sister, and after they left we made love on top of the stove. It rattled, and swarms of cockroaches came rushing out, briefly visible before disappearing into cracks and cupboards.

Wolf took me to Copenhagen for our honeymoon. I had spent so much time in nineteenth-century Denmark that the modern thing was a great disappointment, it was much changed. I was shy speaking Danish in front of Wolf and stumbled over my words. He bought me dozens of Danish books, and a *Little Mermaid* statue. One morning in our hotel, when he was still sleeping, on his stomach, I took the blanket off and looked at him, his slightly wizened and fat back. On one buttock was a dark blue tattoo of a man's face, the man looked in agony. I hadn't noticed it before.

We visited Dyrehavsbakken, the oldest amusement park in the world, and Tivoli Gardens, the second oldest, where we saw a pantomime with Pierrot, Harlequin and Columbine. Wolf said he used to carry Pierrot costumes but that they had stopped selling. He might have some tucked away in the attic or basement, he said. Generally, clowns were not doing very well – the few clown wigs he had on display were dusty. We stopped in Berlin, where he bought a bag of pins and old Soviet fur hats he would sell for three times the price and had shipped home ahead of us.

When we got home, I moved into the costume shop with a suitcase full of my cashmere sweaters, skirts, stockings, my Hans Christian Andersen complete fairy tales, Isak Dinesen in English and in Danish translation – I had written my thesis on her decision to write in English – my Søren Kierkegaards and Jens Peter

Jacobsen's *Niels Lyhne*, and Calico, my cloth doll who had a pair of gold, lensless spectacles glued to her nose.

I was glad to leave my mother's house, it was painted pink, and so narrow we called it 'The Narrow Lady'. It smelled strongly of linseed oil and there were reproductions of Andrei Rublev icons all over the walls and never anything to eat in the cupboards besides mustard powder, rye bread, weak tea bags and oranges from the weak little orange trees my mother grew in light corners of the house. Wolf's fridge was packed with pickled things, cheese, beer, cake, meat and olives.

In Wolf's bedroom, there was a dark wooden bed, with white blankets and pillows. I could tell by the stack of things against one wall that it was a new addition, that the bed he had shared with Eule was different, and now gone. There was a vanity table with a topless Hula girl lamp on it, a spring rocking horse made out of plastic with rusty spring bars, and a hatstand with all Wolf's black hats sitting on it like a bunch of crows. The room was painted purple, and there weren't any windows.

In the backyard was a coach house full of extra mannequins, their hands and heads squashed against the window. There were faded, broken lanterns strung between the coach house and shop, and tangles of rose-bushes with very small pink roses growing on them.

Besides the kitchen and bedroom, there was a living room, full of Wolf's fashion books and other stuff, and a small room he used for sewing and mending and ironing clothes. Wolf's sewing machine was very old, made out of iron. There was always a dress half stuck in it, it looked like an ant eating a piece of lettuce.

The attic became my domain. I removed the moon poster. I found a blue metal trunk to use as a writing desk. I put a fancy metal candlestick on it as the attic light was very weak, a stack of yellow paper, and my Danish dictionary. I wrote by hand.

I still worked in the shop, and Wolf still paid me, but I also knew he kept cash in the Felix the Cat teapot, and I could take as much of it as I wanted, he never said anything.

The weeks leading up to Hallowe'en were the busiest. We opened boxes and boxes of stock: fake wounds, vampire teeth, plastic swords and axes, make-up kits, cotton cobwebs, earrings shaped like jack o'lanterns. Raven wore ghoulish make-up. Wolf hired a few extra people around the store – a woman who wore a witch outfit, I don't think I ever saw her face without make-up, and a tall man who dressed up differently every day – a scarecrow, Frankenstein, some top-hatted character I had never heard of. Wolf, like me, did not dress up. On Hallowe'en eve, the shop stayed open till 9 o'clock – there was always someone who bought a pair of fishnet stockings or an expensive mask last-minute. Then Wolf and I went to bed.

My sister, no longer afraid of Wolf, came into the shop on her free days to borrow things to use in her paintings or to wear to parties. I gave her and mother gifts, pink cashmere sweaters, scarves with foxes on them.

Raven didn't know of the marriage, Wolf's wedding ring wasn't visible amongst all his other rings. Raven treated me with the same disdain he would a clothes moth. Wolf noticed this, and one day Raven was gone and never returned. It was impossible to picture him working anywhere else.

With Raven gone, there was more work, but it was easier, until I found out I was pregnant, not long after Hallowe'en. I realized my youth and my fertility were a large appeal to Wolf. I had somehow thought Wolf was too old to get me pregnant, and so hadn't thought about protection. Wolf didn't buy any new baby things, he had everything we needed stocked away in his basement and backyard shed, as if thirty years ago he had planned for a baby that never came. He gave me some German books: a copy of *Grimm's Fairy Tales* from the 1930s printed on very thin, almost translucent paper written in script, with frightening badly done woodcuts; a copy of *Der Struwwelpeter*; and books by Sibylle von Olfers full of pretty flower children.

I discovered he owned a farmhouse when he told me he was driving out there to pick up a pram. I insisted I go with him. Had he and Eule spent their weekends there? Had they walked around the garden naked, as Germans were said to do?

The drive was the length of the opera *The Magic Flute*, we listened to it on the way there. Wolf drove a very old van with fake leopard skin seat covers. There was a jar of very old pickled eggs in misty water on the dashboard, and crumpled balls of tinfoil from fast food restaurants all over the van floor. The house was red brick with a fallen-in porch and accompanied by a barn with boards missing. They both looked like broken, abandoned pianos.

Wolf said the house was very old and unstable, that the floors and ceilings needed to be fixed, and there could be rodents. I should stay in the car, he didn't want me to get hurt. Once he was inside, I crept around and looked in one of the windows. The windows were dirty, but I saw him squatting, rummaging through boxes – the house was full of boxes – so many boxes it didn't look like a liveable space, it was more like a warehouse.

He left the house, whistling the Queen of the Night Aria and carrying two large bags. The pram was in the barn. It was pale blue, and was covered in bird droppings, but he said he'd wash it.

When the baby was born, he looked like the child of Wolf and Eule: blond, with large features, but he was quiet, like me, so I got on with my Danish novel without much fuss. We named him Wilhelm. Wilhelm looked funny in his old pram, wearing very dated clothes, clutching a Raggedy Ann doll from the 1970s, but many people thought it was quite stylish. My mother didn't approve of my having a baby so young. My sister gave Wilhelm jagged crystals to play with.

One morning, when Wolf was minding the shop, I went into the sewing room which also functioned as his office – he used a corner of the sewing machine desk to do accounts – and found the plastic bags he had picked up at the farm. One had two mannequin heads in it – featureless, unpainted bald ones. The other bag was full of small tin lunchboxes.

I thought at first Wolf had brought them to the city for Wilhelm to use when he was older, but they had pictures of aliens and Bettie Page on them. I also found a black and white photobooth picture of a young Wolf; his hair was long and he had a dramatic animal-tooth earring in his left ear.

Would he have loved me if he was young? Probably not, I thought, and though I wasn't beautiful, there was still a certain shallowness to our age difference: would he love me if I were the same age as him? Probably not. I tucked the photo in my tights.

I opened another tin lunchbox. It was full of vintage sepia and grey pornographic postcards depicting women being spanked or tickled with gigantic ostrich feathers, and other pornographic images from the 1970s, blue, red and orange, and full of hair. Did they belong to Eule or Wolf, or both? A third lunchbox contained a plastic pouch full of grey powder.

I knew that was Eule herself.

.

Finding Eule's ashes filled me with wild thoughts: Wolf would build a shrine to her in the shop, with the ashes in it, or put them in apple pancakes for me to eat so I'd grow to be more like her. Taking Wilhelm for a walk in his pram, I threw the ashes into a public garbage bin, the lunchbox into another. The lunchbox had given me nightmares, that it would start speaking with its lid, like an object in a Disney cartoon, telling me that my sister and I still owed three hundred dollars for that mask my sister broke, and for me to leave her house, but it was gone, and Wolf would never find it.

He went to the farm every few weekends, I sometimes thought he was still looking for Eule's ashes, forgetting he had found them already, since they were gone again. He returned with things that couldn't possibly be whatever he was looking for, a plastic toy ice cream truck missing a wheel he gave to Wilhelm, bowling shirts (we had enough on display in the shop), a case of canned kidney beans which turned out to be expired. He spent more money on gasoline than the worth of the things he returned with.

He filled the attic with boxes of tennis shoes for summer, and musty smelling, thick second-hand bathing suits from the farmhouse. There was no space left for me to comfortably write in the attic, and even with the small window open, the smell of old shoes and swimsuits was overwhelming.

He went on other trips, one to another city to buy a

heap of fur coats and hats from an old Greek man whose fur shop was closing, and another time to Mexico City for a week to buy jewellery. He thought Wilhelm too young to travel, and relied on me to mind the shop and baby. When I had to, I put Wilhelm in the cage with the mannequin wearing a feathered Papageno costume so he wouldn't crawl around and hurt himself, but he would tear at the feathers and eat them.

While Wolf was in Mexico, we received a letter from a historical society of some sort which said the sculptures were ready to be installed. What sculptures? When he returned, he explained that an artist was going to install a historical re-enactment in the shop. The building, our house, was very old, he said, it was a city-wide project to bring history to life. He said business wasn't as good as it used to be: people bought things on the internet. No matter how much variety Wolf had, no matter how far he travelled across the planet in search of wearable treasures, he couldn't compete. The sculptures were already being talked about, the artist who was making them was quite famous. They had signed up for the project a few years before, him and Eule, the artist was one of her favourites.

The other locations were a very old Italian café, a nineteenth-century sewing factory converted into expensive apartments, the Natural History museum, and an underground train stop. The works all depicted gory scenes, as the artist said he wanted to expose the violent side of our country's history.

Wolf was away again on the day the sculptures were installed. They were brought in wooden crate boxes. The artist was a bald man who wore platform creepers and a tiny child's knapsack. Bald heads frightened me, gave me an odd sort of queasiness, a round encyclopaedia of horrible things: crystal balls, marshmallows, testicles, turnips, eggs. I wanted to put one of our wigs on him. He was around Wolf's age and had many assistants. They had floor plans showing where the sculptures were going to go, and consulted each other instead of me. The sculptures were made out of beeswax, like those of Madame Tussaud's.

The first sculpture they unpacked was of a man in nineteenth-century costume with a red beard, holding an axe. The sculpture's brow was furrowed with alarming detail, it was a wax sculpture. The rest of the boxes they brought upstairs.

The artist was unhappy to see a baby, he told me there wasn't one when he accepted this location for the project, and I had better not let the baby touch his artworks. We were responsible if anything happened to his sculptures.

They put two sculptures in our bedroom, consisting of two people each, two moments in time I had to contend with. One, a sexual act, the second, a murder.

In the first a man was penetrating a woman who was on all fours. They had moved the vanity table in our bedroom to make room for it. Like the other man, he had a beard, but a dark brown one. The woman had long black hair, it was all in her face, her gown was over her torso, surrounding her shoulders and head like a flower, her bottom half bare.

The second half of the story was in the corner of the room where our nightstand was. The same woman's dress was cut open, I suppose with the axe, exposing her breasts, which were covered in blood from her throat being slit. She was on her knees, the red bearded man behind her, holding her by the hair. Another man, crouched, fearful and naked in our living room, with a wet drip hanging from his penis. That was the sculpture

163

I hated the most.

In the last scene, in the kitchen, the woman lay on her stomach in a pool of her own blood. The red-haired man was on top of her, in a straddled position. If you squatted and looked closely, you could see that he was inside her, there was synthetic joke-shop faeces and blood on her body. Her dress was gone.

After they had finished installing the sculptures, I took the duvet and pillows off the bed, made a bed in the bathtub, and put Wilhelm's crib in the bathroom too. From then on, Wilhelm and I spent most of our time in the bathroom, we even ate our meals there. The bathroom was the house laid bare, without make-up. It had green tiles with pale brown, wispy flowers on them. The fixtures were old, stained with rust around their orifices. The windowsill and sink were cluttered with bottles of shampoo and soap, razorblades. There was a single framed image on the wall, of a man sitting on a rock, '*Le Génie du Mal* (*Salon de 1838*)' written underneath. He was naked, but was merely pen on paper, he wasn't pink and made to look sweaty like the sculptures. I thought it was a sea man, Neptune, sitting on a rock by the ocean, as he was holding something in one hand that looked like seaweed and had fins in his hair. I thought that for some time, until I looked up the words in a French dictionary. The genius of evil. The glass of the frame was dirty with soap scum. His face could look like Wolf's, if Wolf had a beard.

When Wolf came home he said the sculptures were fantastic. What made him most happy was the throngs of people they brought in, and the amount they bought: they left with fake beards and plastic axes, corsets and suspenders, with gowns and fake blood. My sister came to see them, with a bunch of other students from the art college. I worried my sister admired the sculptures because her own work was so violent, but she pulled me into a corner and said she thought it was different when a man made work like that.

Whenever I walked past the sculptures I covered Wilhelm's eyes. Wolf said Wilhelm wouldn't notice, he was just a baby. He didn't understand that babies were malleable, like butter, and able to absorb all sorts of things.

Children weren't allowed to see the upstairs part of the exhibition, but many came to look, and pose in photographs with the man holding an axe, the man waiting as his future self raped and murdered his wife at the top of the stairs. I went to the library to look up the story: it was all true. Of course, the newspapers from the time didn't report any of the details. I wasn't sure how much research the artist did, and how much he was sensationalizing. The woman, Louise, had only been twenty-three years old when she was killed by her husband. Her husband didn't kill the man she was found with, but chased him onto the streets, naked.

A newspaper did an interview with Wolf, 'who for the past twenty years has run the city's best costume and vintage shop'. There was no mention of me, or Wilhelm. They ran a photo of Wolf standing with his arms crossed beside the man with the axe. When he was home, I slept in our bedroom with him, if only because I was afraid of him becoming titillated by the sculptures, and masturbating at them if I wasn't there to watch him. I slept with the duvet over my head, and wouldn't let him touch me. I left Wilhelm's crib in the bathroom.

The morning after I saw the newspaper article, I woke up very early, and went down to the basement. I turned the furnace up to maximum. It looked like a rusty version of a retro toy robot Wolf had bought for Wilhelm. I was unsure if it would explode or not. I hurriedly put my Danish books, my plain clothes, my manuscript which was much shorter than I wanted it to be, all the cash from the teapot and a jar of pickles in my knapsack and suitcase, and carrying Wilhelm with one arm, walked back to The Narrow Lady. I still had my key.

No one was awake, they didn't hear me come in. I slumped down on the couch, surrounded by dark little paintings of Andrei Rublev and houseplants. A small tree had an orange dangling off one of its branches, the orange was almost the size of a pumpkin, but it was loose and dented looking. I could tell the fruit inside was half the size of its skin, withered to the size of a walnut.

My hair lay in braids on each side of me, Wilhelm curled underneath one of my armpits. There was dry breast milk on the front of my sweater, a ladder leading to a hole in my stockings and one of my boot-laces was untied. I was hungry, but no longer wanted the pickles, it was a mistake to have brought them, the jar was heavy. Instead, I continued to sit there, and thought of the husband that would wake up naked and sweaty to find his young wife and son gone, the sculptures melting and perhaps giving off terrible fumes, the mod podge pictures peeling in the hall, the masks and fur coats becoming warm, the glass countertops covered in condensation, blinding the eyeball rings.

NOTES FROM A SPIDER

These notes were found in a leather binder, written on loose-leaf paper of good quality. The binder was stuffed in an old trunk, underneath a moth-eaten fox fur, small black records, many broken needles, tattered bits of sewn cloth and empty glass medicinal bottles, in a condemned building, the last of many to be torn down to make way for modern and sanitary housing.

I couldn't have been born in any city but this one, a great European capital filled with beautiful, highly detailed architecture, a castle overlooking the river, the city a spread of gilded and copper garlic-like domes, gargoyles, steeples, trains, lampposts resembling moons entrapped by black vines, skylights like dew on buildings, factories, workshops, cabarets, a forest of iron, stone, glass. I certainly can't imagine myself existing in an American or Siberian village, a desert, a valley. I have only seen such places in books, I have never left the city in which I was born. I'm given many invitations to visit villas in foreign countries, castles, the seaside, but I worry I would disappear as soon I stepped out of this city, like a cloud of smog.

I feel part wrought iron, part human and, I won't lie, part vermin.

I have eight legs, and the upper body of a normal man. Black hair, elegant nose and melancholy green eyes, a good set of fake teeth made out of elephants' tusks – I had my real ones removed, like so many gentlemen of my city, so I could enjoy rich food and drink without continual visits to a dentist. I had my fake ones designed to be sharper than my originals, more fang-like. The style has been emulated by many men, young and old.

I bring to mind a spider, an umbrella, a marionette.

The way I move I resemble a large hand with a few extra fingers. I only have one set of genitals – thank goodness! The delicacy and sensation of having a pair between each leg would be unbearable.

The spaces between my other legs resemble armpits, but slightly firmer. They are hairy. I have the hair removed with wax, so there will be less ambiguity when viewing my naked form. I take great care of my feet, each nail covered in clear, shiny polish, each sole dipped in scented powder.

My anus is directly underneath me, my buttocks a circle in the centre of my legs, much like a lavatory on which my torso permanently sits. A chamber pot is much easier for me to use than a modern toilet, and the cafés I patronize regularly provide me with one. Afterwards, I wipe myself with a wet cloth. I take great care with my appearance. I have suits especially made to fit the proportions of my body, though some, including my doctor, have suggested it would be more comfortable for me to wear a gown.

I never wear unmatching shoes, though some people would imagine I would want to, in order to show off my vast collection of footwear. I buy four pairs of each shoe I desire, and wear them all at once.

I could be a stone arabesque that crawled off a building, or a complex contraption belonging to a barber, a photographer or a mathematician. I could be one of many things that exist in the modern city, I play various roles in many fantasies.

It's impossible to imagine my parents, I believe I simply rose out of the city, out of a steamy grate, like Venus out of the ocean. There are many men in the city, deformed by the guns and cannons of the last war, who have only one or two limbs left, or none at all – in a sense they are my fathers. If there is nothing shocking about a man with one limb, what is so shocking about a man with eight?

A soldier with one arm and no other limbs lives on a small wooden wagon outside the metro near my apartments. I always gave him coins until one day he asked if he could have two of my legs instead. He laughed, but his eyes looked so envious, so hungry, that I never stopped to give him anything again. I scurried away on my infinitely precious eight feet, an abundance of flesh.

From what I was told, I was left on a church doorstep, like a gargoyle that had fallen from its façade. I was brought to an orphanage, but I was too exceptional to stay in an orphanage long, news spread of me quickly. A handful of kind, curious patrons hired a nanny to raise me, tutors to educate me, a doctor to watch my health carefully. I was a particular favourite among wealthy women. No one person possessed me, I was considered a child of the city. Everyone important visited, brought me toys, books, musical instruments.

Though I wasn't forced to learn a specific skill, or to heighten my difference with strange tricks, like the circus dwarf who is taught to juggle and dance, I played piano a little, had a fine voice, and knew arithmetic. But I knew from a young age that I would mainly devote myself to pleasures of less effort: to eating, drinking, reading, loving.

My legs are somewhat weak, long but childlike, despite exercises especially designed by my doctor. It is necessary that I walk with a cane. I have one with a silver spider on the handle.

With women, I often oblige them to sit astride me so that I won't be overly weakened. I sleep the way a flower does, closed like an umbrella.

I have many women friends, and many woo me. One, a rich baron's wife, had a coat made out of insects' fur for me. She had hundreds of tarantulas and bees killed in order to make it, in order to appeal to me, but never have I been so repulsed. I care deeply for the creatures so many others despise: spiders, moths, rats, mice, all manners of bugs. They are my kind.

I have two pet rats, one white, one black, Odilon and Claude, whom I take with me everywhere in a leather and gold cage. I feed them candied almonds, bits of sausage and oranges. They are fond of me, they love to crawl across my many limbs, and I have my suits made with a few extra inches of loose fabric so that they can comfortably sit between my legs and the cloth. People often mistake their lumpish outlines for further deformations of my body, and are horrified when they move.

I am the city's muse. Many artists have painted me, and there is a sculpture of my body, nude except for a bowler hat, in a public garden, upon a pedestal, with a poem, written in my honour, carved into it.

An architect designed a glass and steel pavilion full of palms where one can have tea, topped with a bronze model of my head, and a round theatre, made of black and white marble, the black marble designed in arches emulating my legs.

I also make a substantial amount doing advertisements for: absinthe, shaving lotion, wafers, sparkling water, brogues, bowties, soap, feather dusters, jewellery, truffles, silk, macaroons, liquorice, typewriters, photography studios, paint, thread, tea, perfume, coffee, Bergamot oil, sock garters, galoshes, tinned oysters, umbrellas, moustache wax, fishnet stockings, walking canes, bowler hats and nougat.

I refuse to do advertisements for insecticide, though

I have been asked many times. How I hate those horrible shops with rats nailed to the façade, boxes of poison, traps for creatures of all sizes, some so large they might catch an unfortunate child.

How I love cockroaches, lice, fleas, pigeons, moths, rats, mice, spiders, sparrows and of course, *cimex lectularius*. It is thanks to me such dwellers in this city have a safe haven. Using my vast funds, I created a zoo where a selection of so-called vermin can exist in fascinating proliferation, in a closed-off area of the city, where glass tunnels have been built so that human citizens may walk through unmolested and unbitten. Visitors bring them rotten meat, stale bread, old clothes and bedding. Some find it relaxing, even addictive, to watch the creatures propagate, consume, die, to see them exist in a space where they can do each without restraint, without poison, brooms, traps, felines and dogs.

From a distance, my zoo resembles a great gallery or train station. It has many glass roofs, and grand pediments with friezes depicting rodents and insects. At the entrance, there is a bronze statue of me, a rat in one hand, a moth in the other.

I love the moth house, for those creatures consume everything. The moths were enclosed in a structure resembling a greenhouse. Every morning a man who wears an outfit similar to a beekeeper's opens one of the glass panels and throws in a bag of stale bread and a pile of coats. In such profusion, the swarms of moths resemble swathes of brown fabric or vicious and strange tropical trees which sway to an unknown breeze.

Inside the rat house is a model in miniature of our city, the very same buildings and streets, so that one may watch the rats, so man-like with their hands and whiskers, go about their business of breeding, eating

173

and digesting. The cockroaches and mice keep themselves hidden under old mattresses and couches. If one taps the glass of their cage with a cane or a fist, they move from one hiding place to another, storms of brown and grey. I always bring along a pair of opera glasses, to view the fleas and bed bugs.

The spider house is quiet. It has so many webs it resembles an arctic landscape in its whiteness. It is still except for the morning feeding, when flies and other small creatures are sacrificed. There is a great difference to me between a spider that needs blood, and so must kill, and the unnecessary crushing of spiders, simply because we do not like the sight of their webs in our windowsills. The spinning of webs in the zoo is barely perceptible to the viewer, but the spiders communicate with each other by playing their webs like string instruments, a harmonious music you can hear when all else is silent. They are common household spiders, from the windowsills and corners of my city. Some auspicious women visit the zoo specifically for the spiders, almost praying to them, telling them their secrets and their ailments, as if their words will be absorbed into the webs. I heard that some younger women bring, hidden in precious boxes, the pulp of their menstruation to give to the spiders, believing that doing so will bring them love, marriage, children, and even death. The zookeeper has shown me such boxes, like the ones rings are held in, but stained with blood. He keeps them in his office, after dropping the blood clots into the spiders' home.

I also draw such attentions. Women unsatisfied with their husbands and unable to bear children come to my apartments begging. I sometimes oblige if their gifts for me are exquisite enough – a fur stole, or a crate of pomegranates or blood oranges, each fruit wrapped in gold foil, for example. The children that result all have my distinguished face, but none my multiple legs. Some women were too nervous and excitable when they saw me naked, my phallus extended like a ninth leg. The women most capable of dealing with an array of different bodies were prostitutes. They told me about the hundreds of deformities hidden under men's clothing. They were never surprised nor shocked. Publicly, I spent most of my time with actresses and opera singers. I had my own box at all the theatres and opera houses in the city. I always wore a long black cape and sat in the back of my boxes, half hidden in the shadows so as not to draw attention away from the performances. I was the most famous man in my city, my face was everywhere. I was like a monument so large you could see it from wherever you were standing. There was even a ballet and an opera written about me. The ballet was titled *Son of Arachne*, the opera *The Black Spider*.

I have been asked to take to the stage myself, but my health would not permit it. It would be too exhausting on top of all my other activities.

It was after the premiere of *Son of Arachne*, however, that I fell into despair. For the *pas de deux*, a male and female wore tutus designed to look like multiple legs. (Ah, that female equivalent of me that doesn't exist!) How they danced together, while I faced life alone! I bought a female tarantula from an exotic menagerie and kept her in a glass box shaped like a palace, I slept with four prostitutes all at once to immerse myself in a tangle of female legs, and later, I borrowed the costume from the ballet and made one of the women wear it, but nothing satisfied me. I went for long drives in my carriage at night, the carriage itself was spider-like, I had its lace curtains designed to look like webs. I was searching, it seemed impossible that this city of factories, of specialist shops, this city that could produce everything in great quantities could only produce one of me. I stopped in front of Gothic cathedrals and ornate balconies, hoping for a mistress who resembled me to crawl down from their heights.

On one such night, driving across a shopping boulevard where the shop window lights were kept on all night, I spotted the most beautiful but inhuman thigh and told my driver to stop. It was a sewing machine shop. The machine in the window had four legs, like iron plants, a wooden body, a swan-like curved metal neck and a circular platform to run the fabric across, not unlike the plate on a gramophone where the record is placed, and a small mouth with one silver tooth. She was an unusual, modern creature. What beautiful music she must make! Florence was her name, it was stencilled on the shop window. FLORENCE. I sat there in my carriage until it was morning and the shop opened. I hastily purchased her, the one in the window. They asked if I wanted her taken apart for carrying, but I had her put, as is, in my carriage. I drove through the city, my legs entwined with hers, two of my feet placed on her sole-shaped pedals.

The shop owners gave me a catalogue of sewing machines, all the names tantalizing: Cleopatra, Countess, Dolly Varden, Daisy, Elsa, Alexandra, Diamond, Gloria, Little Gem, Godiva, Jennie June, Pearl, Victoria, Titania, Princess Beatrice, Penelope, Queen Mab, Empress, Anita, Bernina, Little Wonder, but none more than my Florence, sitting across from me.

Back at my apartments, I tried to bring her to life. I put a hankie from my pocket below her mouth, I fed her string, the very best, I pressed the pedal, but she was stubborn. She swore at me in large, uneven stitch-es, harsh lines on my kerchief. I wept. I embraced her desperately, kissing the metal body, but she was frigid and still.

Florence needed a woman to assist her, a lady in wait-ing, she was telling me. I asked one of my servants to call one of the prostitutes I saw regularly, and to bring her over in my carriage as soon as possible. Her name was Polina and her black, curly hair reminded me of Florence's legs.

After she undressed, I told her to sit at the machine, and sew.

She pressed the pedal and laughed, blowing me a kiss. She got up and tried to join me on my chaise, but I demanded she sit down by Florence again. She pout-ed, and said what use did she have for knowing how to use a sewing machine? Her Madame fixed her under-things when they were torn. It wouldn't do! I needed a professional, a seamstress. I told Polina to get out. I immediately wrote an ad for a newspaper and sent it by telegraph so it would appear the next morning.

WANTED

SEAMSTRESS

Oh those poor thin bespectacled things who lived in basements and attics, living off thin soup and dented cans of fish, their backs hunched, their fingers thin and calloused. Yes, there was something insect-like about them. I interviewed many, and settled on a young thing, not yet deformed by her profession. Her hair was the same chestnut colour as Florence's wooden torso. I had her measured, and a dress made of black lace that fol-lowed the same pattern as Florence's legs. I bought rolls of white, black and gold silk, for Florence to speak to me with.

The girl blushed when she changed into the dress, one could easily see her breasts and bottom through the pattern. I sat close by, and told her to sit down with Florence, and begin.

Ah, those stitches, like lipstick marks left on a paper napkin, sweet poems. The girl worked and worked, caressing Florence in a beautiful dance. I clutched the finished sheets of clothes to my chest. I didn't want the girl to stop, I closed the curtains. We both became hypnotized, I don't know how much time passed, but I watched and watched, telling the girl, 'Do not stop, do not stop!' in quick breaths until the girl collapsed, the cloth becoming tangled, Florence's mouth slowing until it was still.

Florence, my mistress, had killed the seamstress.

My stove was more decorative than utilitarian, a green and black box with as many ornamental figures and faces as an opera house. I had my meals in restaurants and didn't use the stove for more than heating sugar, and it took all day to burn the remnants of the seamstress, whom I chopped up into little morsels no bigger than mussels, taking off the dress I had made for her first, of course, and draping it carefully over Florence, to whom it really belonged.

I was tempted, many times, to take the seamstress's body to my zoo. Oh, how the rats, moths and fleas would consume her in a moment.

I had spent days, nights, in the company of Florence and the seamstress, unaware of time passing. After the seamstress's body was burned, I was famished, greatly weakened. I kissed Florence and went to a restaurant. I ate my meal quickly, I was impatient to get back to

Florence, but I needed another seamstress. I couldn't use the same newspaper.

I waited near a clothing factory in my carriage and as the girls went home, I stopped and talked to one that appealed to me, the same chestnut hair, the same size as my first seamstress, so that I could reuse the dress I had. I gave the girl a meal delivered from a restaurant before she began, so that she would last longer, but not a meal heavy enough to make her lethargic.

I read the swathes of cloth, her fine, straight stitches, a mysterious and invigorating language, a great novel of love for me. I wrapped myself in them. I only left the apartment to eat, to find more seamstresses, to buy more cloth.

In Florence's honour, I would open a sewing machine museum, which would also provide me with a steady stream of seamstresses. I would call it the Florentina Museum, an iron and glass building resembling a magnificent web. My patronesses loved the idea, though they had never sewn themselves. It would be recognition of women's work, and they gave me the money I needed. The museum was planned under my direction, and sewing machine manufacturers donated models and further funds.

The seamstresses came to the museum on weekends in droves, either out of a strange curiosity to see machines unlike the ones they worked with or because they were scared of being away from their machines. No one would love them, so they pushed their affection towards the very machines that destroyed them. They didn't have sewing machines at home, they couldn't afford them. Simple needles and threads wouldn't do, and so they came to my museum in their free hours, their lonely hearts longing to see a treadle, a wheel. The machines had disfigured the seamstresses, they put all their beauty and youth into dresses, curtains and suits. It was easy to spot them, the pale skin, the tired eyes with purple half-circles underneath like violent-tinted spectacles, the squinting, their fingers worn thin, almost needles themselves, hidden in cheap gloves, the shaking legs that would have been muscly from pumping had they had more meat to eat.

The museum had a café, where I now went every weekend for anise and pistachio éclairs and coffee in small black and gold cups. The seamstresses sat at the arabesque iron café tables, their legs moving up and down underneath. They wore hats and shoes made out of black cardboard and carried little pouches filled with iron pills or tonic, often given to them by their factories to keep them alive, and took them with their coffee.

'If you could do a quick sewing job for me, I have a machine, some silk pyjamas that have ripped, what fine fingers you have, I will pay you of course, and give you dinner too, a fine steak, some roast chicken.'

They lost track of time, there were no clocks in my apartment for this purpose, the curtains were shut, the air was heavy from the stove and gas lamps. I worked them for days and they became hypnotized, as did I, watching the beautiful iron limbs of Florence move.

But the point came when, watching the girls wilt with exhaustion, watching the machine consume them, feeling the cloth covered in gold, black, green and red stitches wasn't enough any longer. I wanted to be involved in the process, to be *touched* by Florence.

I cut open my leg with a pen knife and said to the current seamstress sitting in front of Florence, a weak thing with a thin black braid, 'Sew it, sew it up, my dear. No, there is no need to call a physician, just sew it up for me, dear, on the machine.'

Without wiping the blood away, I stuck one of my legs underneath, pale with black hairs, like a roll of cloth that had been slept on, and commanded the seamstress to sew, the cold metal of Florence's flesh poised above me. What relief, what joy, what pain with the first stitch!

They were love bites, to me. They weren't as legible or as even as the stitches on cloth, but just as beautiful.

Soon, all eight of my legs were covered in stitches and scars, like a ragdoll, Florence's kisses. The loss of blood weakened me immensely. I started to walk with two canes instead of one, and I partook of iron pills and tonics, just as the seamstresses did. I barely had any appetite for food, I was too lovesick. For my visits to the zoo, I bought a wheeled chaise which one of my servants pushed me in, but otherwise I did not leave my apartments, I refused invitations, no longer did any modelling. Only my creatures in the zoo understood, I thought, my consuming desire for Florence, my endless hunger for cloth covered in her stitches, for her stitches in my flesh. I brought a bag of wigs for the moths, sausages for the rats, and a cage full of kittens for the fleas. I watched them eat, then returned home.

The few times I had visitors over between seamstresses, so as not to raise too many suspicions as I had previously been so sociable, I covered Florence with a cloth. I didn't want them to see something so intimate to me.

Disposing of used seamstresses was exhausting. I bought a larger stove, saying I suffered more and more from the cold. I couldn't even ask my servants for help. I let go all but one, who drove my carriage. Visiting my doctor, I was reluctant for him to see my legs. I told him I was attacked by the dog of a woman friend. My doctor told me I had to stop seeing her at once, and to stay away from dogs. I couldn't afford to lose more blood, I needed more than the average person with my extra appendages; my heart was overworked.

Oh indeed it was, but he did not know how much.

He was disgusted by my stitches. What awful, back-door surgeon had I visited and why? Why did I not visit him, my trusted doctor since childhood? He gave me a bottle of antiseptic liquid to put on the wounds. I vowed never to visit him again.

I had piles of telegrams, invitations, letters, news-papers, but the only thing I read was Florence's cloth, yes, and her lovebites, I think she is beginning to love me, I feed her, she writes she writes

The last page ends with an indeterminate smudge, whether blood, ink or alcohol, it is too aged for the naked eye to determine.

Acknowledgements

Thank you, Nicola. Thank you Sasha, Shaunna, Anna, Emma. Thank you to Josie at *Granta*, and to Francesca at *The White Review*. Thank you very much to Fitzcarraldo Editions.

Box Hill by Adam Mars-Jones (Fiction)
'An exquisitely discomfiting tale of a submissive same-sex relationship... perfectly realised.'
— Anthony Cummins, *Observer*

A Girl's Story by Annie Ernaux (Essay)
Translated by Alison L. Strayer
'A profound and beautiful examination of the impenetrable wall that time erects between the self we are, and the selves we once were. I know of no other book that so vividly illustrates the frustrations and the temptations of that barrier, and our heartache and longing in trying to breach it.'
— Sheila Heti, author of *Motherhood*

Grove by Esther Kinsky (Fiction)
Translated by Caroline Schmidt
'What makes *Grove* so noteworthy is the keening, perfectly weighted clarity of Esther Kinsky's prose; Caroline Schmidt's elegantly considered translation is meticulous but never overstated.'
— Lucy Scholes, *Financial Times*

Minor Detail by Adania Shibli (Fiction)
Translated by Elisabeth Jaquette
'An extraordinary work of art, *Minor Detail* is continuously surprising and absorbing: a very rare blend of moral intelligence, political passion and formal virtuosity.'
— Pankaj Mishra, author of *The Age of Anger*

Index Cards by Moyra Davey (Essay)
'*Index Cards* is an essential portrait of an artist wide open to the world and ever-in-formation: reading (always reading, the undertow of her practice), looking, suffering, talking, loving – preparing to make work and risking the making of it. I could not put it down.'
— Kate Briggs, author of *This Little Art*

Rave by Rainald Goetz (Fiction)
Translated by Adrian Nathan West
'This is writing of and from the body, hot, sweaty, dazed, decadent, and ultimately life-affirming.'
—— Julia Bell, author of *The Dark Light*

King Kong Thoery by Virginie Despentes (Essay)
Translated by Frank Wynne
'I can think of almost no book I've enjoyed in recent years as much as *King Kong Theory*... In a world that continues to have difficulty contending with sex work, porn, class, and sexual violence without resorting to tired tropes, Virginie Despentes offers a fresh, necessary, inspiring path forward, just as she has been doing for decades now in a variety of media. This book is a classic, and I'm so grateful for it.'
—— Maggie Nelson, author of *The Argonauts*

The Appointment by Katharina Volckmer (Fiction)
'Surprising, inventive, disturbing and beautiful – *The Appointment* is an overdue, radical intervention.'
—— Chris Kraus, author of *I Love Dick*

Suppose a Sentence by Brian Dillon (Essay)
'Dillon has brilliantly reinvented the commonplace book in this witty, erudite, and addictively readable guide to the sentences that have stayed with him over the years.'
—— Jenny Offill, author of *Weather*

I is Another: Septology III-V by Jon Fosse (Fiction)
Translated by Damion Searls
'The reader of *I is Another* is both on the riverbank and in the water being carried forward, and around, by the great, shaping, and completely engrossing, flow of Fosse's words. It's a doubleness of view that is reflected in the characters, named Asle, who are both one and other, and through which we can see and feel the world, and ourselves, more clearly.'
—— David Hayden, author of *Darker with the Lights On*

A Man's Place by Annie Ernaux (Essay)
Translated by Tanya Leslie
'Ernaux has inherited de Beauvoir's role of chronicler to a generation.'
— Margaret Drabble, *New Statesman*

rein GOLD by Elfriede Jelinek (Essay)
Translated by Gitta Honegger
'In *rein GOLD*, Jelinek reimagines the characters of Brünnhilde and Wotan from Wagner's Ring cycle and transposes them into the context of modernity. She delivers an impassioned exposé of the discontents of capitalism. Her musical thought is interwoven with myth, politics, and Wagnerian motifs. Gitta Honegger's excellent translation allows us to experience the intense flow of her characters' streams of consciousness entangled in greed and alienation.'
— Xiaolu Guo, author of *A Lover's Discourse*

Bolt from the Blue by Jeremy Cooper (Fiction)
'*Bolt from the Blue* is a scintillating, wistful exploration of a good career and a poor relationship. Pithy yet expansive, it's an essential, engrossing, illuminating read for any aspiring artist.'
— Sara Baume, author of *Handiwork*

In Memory of Memory by Maria Stepanova (Essay)
Translated by Sasha Dugdale
'The poet Maria Stepanova's *In Memory of Memory*, beautifully translated by Sasha Dugdale, is a deeply intelligent quest for the significance of minutiae that survive while grand narratives of history sweep over them. It makes for powerful and magical reading, reminiscent of Nabokov's *Speak Memory*. Time and again the sheer richness of the task sustains us and drives us on. This is a wholly marvellous book that extends our knowledge of all that is valued and lost.'
— George Szirtes, author of *The Photographer at Sixteen*

Simple Passion by Annie Ernaux (Essay)
Translated by Tanya Leslie
'A work of lyrical precision and diamond-hard clarity.'
— *New Yorker*

The Things We've Seen by Agustín Fernández Mallo (Fiction)
Translated by Thomas Bunstead
'There are certain writers whose work you turn to knowing you'll find extraordinary things there. Borges is one of them, Bolaño another. Agustín Fernández Mallo has become one, too. This novel, which ranges across the world and beyond it, is hugely ambitious in scope. It's a weird, recursive, paranoiac, funny, menacing and thrilling book.'
— Chris Power, author of *A Lonely Man*

Fifty Sounds by Polly Barton (Essay)
'Witty, exuberant, also melancholy, and crowded with intelligence – *Fifty Sounds* is so much fun to read. Barton has written an essay that is also an argument that is also a prose poem. Let's call it a slant adventure story, whose hero is equipped only with high spirits, and a ragtag band of phonemes.'
— Rivka Galchen, author of *Everyone Knows Your Mother Is a Witch*

Subscribe to Fitzcarraldo Editions:
fitzcarraldoeditions.com/subscribe

Fitzcarraldo Editions
8-12 Creekside
London, SE8 3DX
United Kingdom

ISBN 978-1-910695-37-1

Design by Ray O'Meara
Typeset in Fitzcarraldo
Printed and bound by TJ Books

Fitzcarraldo Editions